A Little Friendly Advice

Siobhan Vivian

PUSH

SCHOLASTIC INC.

NEW YORK TORONTO LONDON AUCKLAND SYDNEY
MEXICO CITY NEW DELHI HONG KONG BUENOS AIRES

No part of this publication may be reproduced, or stored in a retrieval system, or transmitted in any form or by any means, electronic, mechanical, photocopying, recording, or otherwise, without written permission of the publisher. For information regarding permission, write to Scholastic Inc., Attention: Permissions Department, 557 Broadway, New York, NY 10012.

ISBN-13: 978-0-545-00405-3
ISBN-10: 0-545-00405-5

Text copyright © 2008 by Siobhan Vivian.

All rights reserved. Published by PUSH, an imprint of Scholastic Inc.

SCHOLASTIC and associated logos are trademarks and/or registered trademarks of Scholastic Inc.

12 11 10 9 8 7 6 5 4 3 2 1   9 10 11 12 13 14/0

Printed in the U.S.A.   40

First PUSH paperback printing, March 2009

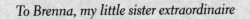

To Brenna, my little sister extraordinaire

ACKNOWLEDGMENTS

David Levithan, editor/mentor/friend/G.O.M. I can't thank you enough for everything you've done, but I sure will try. You are my light. Here's to endless *this* and *that*.

Extra sparkly kudos to the hardworking folks at Scholastic. I greatly appreciate all your efforts.

Rosemary Stimola, my agent and fellow Jersey girl. Thanks for your wisdom, guidance, and sass.

I offer everlasting high fives to those who wielded red pen, gave their unwavering support, and prevented me from hurling my laptop out the window—Kathryne B. Alfred, Coe Booth, Daphne Grab, Lisa Graff, Lisa Greenwald, Jenny Han, Caroline Hickey, TEAM FRIENDSHIP (Sara Shandler and Lynn Weingarten), Eamon Tobin, my best friend, Erin Comaskey, and Sarah Weeks and Tor Seidler of The New School MFA Creative Writing program.

Brian Carr, thanks for dropping everything to read my newest pages. Operation Omega forever.

Nick Caruso, I'm so grateful for all the love, support, and impromptu dance parties you've given me. xoxo.

Mom and Dad, you are the Best. Parents. Ever. Your tennis court and swimming pool are in the mail.

ONE

The wrapping paper on my birthday present is impenetrable. Mom must have used half a roll of tape to secure the sharp folds, creases, and delicate trimmings just so. She wants my Sweet Sixteen to be special — more special than me wearing a Hanes undershirt, Levi's, and my dirty pair of Converse in our cramped mustard-yellow kitchen.

"I bet you can't even fit into that pretty sundress I bought you in August!" Mom taunted when she realized I was dead serious about not dressing up for dinner. "You've shot up at least three more inches since then."

It was endearingly pathetic. So I put on a foil party crown.

Mom cooked her homemade ziti, got me a whale-shaped ice-cream cake with chocolate crunchies from the Carvel across town, and invited my friends over at nine to help me blow out the candles. Once we're all tweaked out on sugar, we're going to bail on Mom for some suburban debauchery in my honor. Even though it's Thursday, I'm allowed out until midnight.

"Dinner was awesome," I say, and watch Mom's lean body shake with elbow grease as she scrubs hardened noodles off a Pyrex dish. A chocolate-brown ponytail swishes across her shoulder blades and a few gray hairs catch the light from overhead. They seem to sparkle.

"The trick is, I cut all the ingredients in half . . . except for the cheese," Mom tells me over the sound of running sink water. She is a pro at halving family-sized recipes. The anti–Betty Crocker.

I shake her present next to my ear. It doesn't make a sound. "Can't you do the dishes later?"

"All this buildup. The suspense must be killing you!" When she turns around, her grin is wide. She flings a damp dish towel over her shoulder and plops into the seat across from me. "Happy birthday, Ruby."

I tear into the package, prepared to give an Oscar-worthy performance of Best Reaction to a Bad Present. Historically, Mom has exploited gift-buying opportunities as chances to make me more girly. A baby-blue eyelet blouse with cap sleeves to soften my angular boyish figure. A palette of sparkly eye shadows to brighten my strikingly plain face. Some dangly earrings that get swallowed up by my dark, thick hair. I never begrudge her thinly veiled makeover attempts. It just seems stupid to keep things I'm never going to use. So I trade the goods for credit at the thrift store and get presents more my style. Like old camp T-shirts from summers before I was born, jeans so worn you could trace the white outline of the pocket where the previous owner's wallet was kept, or those striped socks that have little sections for each of your toes.

But Mom promised this year would be different. That I was going to "absolutely die" when I saw her present. She's been all goofy over finally cracking the code to her daughter's weirdness, a proud moment for a single parent whose kid turned out to be nothing like her. I only hope I can act my way out of disappointing her. After all, she's trying. And trying should count for something.

"Read the card! The card!" Mom says, rescuing it from the shreds of wrapping paper I've tossed aside. But I'm already inside the box. When I unfold the flaps of tissue, my mouth drops open and I swallow the whole roomful of air in surprise.

My hands hold an old Polaroid camera. It's tan and black, with three retro racing stripes of red, yellow, and blue darting down the front. There's a tower of four flashcubes, like miniature disco balls stacked on top of each other. A nylon lariat threads through a loop of plastic on the back. I slip it over my head and the cord digs into the back of my neck. It feels wonderfully clunky.

"I found it at the camera shop on West Market. I wanted to splurge on one of those digital cameras, but once I spotted this on a shelf behind the register, I knew you'd get a real kick out of it. The man said it's in perfect condition, though it took me half a roll of paper towels to wipe away all the dust." She reaches underneath the tissue and hands me two boxes of film, which she explains are standard and still available at CVS.

It takes a few tries, but I figure out how to load the film into the front hatch. Then I frame Mom's face in the viewfinder and pull the orange trigger. The room flashes and the camera roars. Seconds later, it spits out a foggy white square.

I've never owned a real camera before. Just those cheap disposables you can buy at the drugstore. I didn't even know I wanted one. It's not like many moments in my life are picture worthy. But now that I do, well . . . it couldn't be a more perfect present.

"Mom," I say, but she cuts me off with a *shhh* before I can get sappy. We are very anti-sap.

"Here. You're supposed to at least *pretend* like you're interested in this." Mom replaces the photo in my hand with an envelope. She's not annoyed or anything. I can tell by the way she's grinning.

The card is her plain cream-colored stationery, folded once along the middle. There's no flowery Hallmarkian poem with twirly golden script about how I'm now a real woman and blah-blah-barf. I am so thankful that hormone-soaked sentiment is not our relationship. It just makes things uncomfortable. Especially with a history like ours.

I crack it open.

Ruby,

Make wonderful memories.

Love, Mom

I look up at her and smile, but she's already returned to dish duty. Her photograph lies on the table. Even partially developed, my mom is so pretty — a stark contrast from the peeling linoleum of our kitchen floor, a stark contrast from me.

The doorbell rings. Three times, rapid fire.

"Now, who on earth could that be?" Mom asks in a sugary way. She peers over her shoulder and winks, because we both already know.

I run out of the kitchen, hurdle the living room coffee table, and position myself steps away from our front door. Raising the camera to my eye, I fight to keep the laughter inside my mouth. "It's open!"

Beth is wearing a green mohair cardigan over a gray tank top, dark skinny jeans, and pointy brown leather flats. The sides of her wavy auburn hair are pinned back with a few bobby pins and her face is tinged pink from her brisk walk around the block. She steps into my house but freezes in action pose as the flash pops.

"Surprise!" I shout, before she can wish me a happy birthday for the fiftieth time today. Beth was the first to call me, at exactly 12:01 A.M. She bought me a birthday egg-and-cheese bagel and delivered it to my homeroom. She covered my locker with pictures of birthday cakes from an old cookbook, threw two fists of three-hole-punch confetti on me at the lunch table, and forced me to tie a helium balloon to the strap of my book bag and keep it there for the entire day.

"Ruby!" she screams and lunges with wiggling peach-polished fingers. I am seven inches taller than Beth, so I hold the photo over my head, comically out of her reach. But she's not afraid to exploit my weakness. She jabs a finger into my armpit and I recoil in a fit of laughter.

I hustle backward to the kitchen and Beth makes chase. We circle the table and both of us are screaming and laughing so hard the windows shake in their frames. Beth slows down only to kiss my mom hello on the cheek.

I am way out of breath, so I stop. Beth throws her arms around my neck and sinks us to the floor. We stare at the photo in my hands. As our panting subsides, her face emerges from the mist of the film. Her hazel eyes are wide open and her mouth is a perfect O.

"Ha! I look like you!" she says, because I'm notorious for making stupid faces in pictures while everyone else around me smiles like normal.

"No, you don't," I say, pointing to the gap in my front teeth. A genetic gift from my dad that I absolutely hate. It's wide enough to slide a nickel through, like I'm a human slot machine. Beth's teeth are naturally perfect. She's never had braces or even any cavities. They're all tiny and straight and white, like Chiclets. I stick my tongue out at her.

"I like your little space," she says. "It's cute."

I roll my eyes. "You think everything is cute. Even dog poop."

"Shut up! Dog poop can be cute," she says, matter-of-factly. "But not as cute as rabbit poop." We both laugh and my mom calls us crazy.

The doorbell rings.

"Ooh! That's Katherine!" Beth says, glancing at the clock over the sink. "Her mom was going to drop her off after her basketball game."

She wants us to surprise Katherine with another guerrilla picture, but suddenly I'm worried about conserving my film. That, and Katherine gets on my nerves. But Beth is so excited, hopping up and down like a little kid who has to pee, I shrug and follow her lead.

Beth readies her hand on the brass knob and I crouch down near the recliner. The bell rings again, this time long and impatient. As Beth swings the door open, I spring up like a jack-in-the-box. We both scream our heads off.

The flash pops, but Katherine doesn't even blink. Instead, she leans against the door frame in her yellow track pants and

6

navy Akron High School varsity basketball sweatshirt. Her chapped lips wrinkle around a brown filter, and she takes the last deep drag of her cigarette before casting it off into my neighbor's bushes.

"I could seriously kill my parents," she says. A combination of smoke and her hot breath in the cold air clouds her face.

The three of us head into the kitchen while Katherine rambles off a crazy recap of her parents fighting in the bleachers over who will keep which half of their sectional sofa. Beth gets her a glass of water. I quietly watch the picture develop in my hands. With her stick-straight blonde hair and icy blue eyes, Katherine is too pretty to be a smoker.

Beth taps Katherine on the shoulder to scoot in her chair because she wants to help my mom push the candles into my cake. It's a tight squeeze past the sink, and Katherine moves in, but not nearly enough for Beth to pass. Rather than ask again, Beth goes around the other way. I don't think Katherine even notices. She just looks around the room in wide-eyed wonder.

"Wow, this is like the smallest kitchen I've ever seen."

Oh, right. The new girl's never been in my house before.

"Yeah, well . . ." I say, but decide not to get into it. Anyhow, she's right. The kitchen is tiny. We have to keep the refrigerator in the pantry and our oven filled with pots and pans. When I want an English muffin or a frozen waffle, I have to move the block of knives over to the table so there's room for the toaster on the tiny spread of countertop. It's nowhere near the size of the kitchen in our old house. But Katherine wouldn't know that.

Katherine's only been hanging out with us for a few weeks, since Beth found her crying on the windowsill in the girls' bathroom during fourth period. She said that none of her friends understood what she was going through, now that her dad had officially decided to move out. Apparently, Katherine tried to have a heart-to-heart with a few of her teammates on the way to a basketball game. The girls half listened to her sad story, between joking with each other and waving to the cars passing by the team bus. When Katherine was finished, they reminded her that, as both captain and their strongest player, she had to concentrate on the court if Akron High was going to squeak out a victory against Barberton. So Katherine pushed everything out of her mind and played her best game of the season. Her teammates congratulated her on the win, then boarded the bus, put on their headphones, and rode back without another word. No one cared about her family problems, so long as she made her free throws. And that's when she decided that she needed some new friends.

That day, at fifth period lunch, Beth told us the story. I found it weird that Katherine would admit all that to a relative stranger, but whatever. Beth said that we couldn't turn our backs on her, even if Katherine wasn't quite a perfect fit with our established group dynamic.

"Says who?" I had taunted in my best wise-ass voice when Beth had brought it up. Maria had laughed at that. And even Beth had cracked a smile. After all, it wasn't like we were looking to increase our numbers. The addition of Maria to our twosome last year, when the principal assigned Beth to be her shadow, caused me enough stress. Sure, it all turned out fine in the end. Maria was into the same kind of things we were — thrift stores, rock music, and rolling our eyes over how dumb the popular kids were. But I still had growing pains and all the other awkward stuff that comes with getting used to someone new. Katherine was a different story altogether. We had nothing in common with her. She was a senior, and we were all sophomores. She was popular (or at least she used to be), athletic, and pretty wild. We were, well, not. I just had a feeling that Katherine wouldn't be worth the trouble.

But later, at my locker, Beth had pushed my brown hair aside and had whispered into my ear. She reminded me that I knew more than anyone what Katherine was going through with her family stuff. She said there was probably a lot I could do to help her.

I felt like a real jerk. Especially with how great Beth had been to me, single-handedly helping me survive all my own family drama. I couldn't imagine what kind of state I'd have been in if I hadn't had a friend like her looking out for me. So I've been trying, mostly for Beth. But for Katherine too, I guess. Though she doesn't make it easy.

Gravel crunches under a set of tires in the driveway. I grab my camera again and return to the door. This time, I drop to the carpet and point the Polaroid out of our mail slot. As Maria walks up the stairs, I snap a picture. Her knees are brown and meaty and partially concealed by red stripey leg warmers.

Maria blows me an air kiss and sheds her fur-collared old lady coat as she walks though the door, shifting her cell phone from ear to ear. "You can't come! I told you, NO BOYS TONIGHT!" she shouts before flipping her phone closed and rolling her eyes. "Ugh, he is so annoying!"

I nod in sympathy, but the truth is, Maria talks to so many guys, I have no idea which *he* she's currently annoyed with. Maybe it's this guy Davey who graduated last year and works at Square Records. I spotted her draped all over him in the school parking lot yesterday, while I was walking toward the science wing for a lunchtime study session.

I doubt they saw me. I'm very quiet.

"Cool camera! It's a certifiable relic!" Maria says, batting her long eyelashes and raking her fingers through her choppy little bangs. She leans in and whispers in my ear. "Meanwhile, you are totally in for some major birthday madness tonight! So let's down the family cake and get going, okay?"

I skip back into the kitchen. On the way, the lights go out. Mom sets the glowing cake in front of an empty seat at the table. I sit and look out at the four bodies that fill the tiny room. Beth snaps my picture with my new camera and, for once, I smile as big and bright and normal as I can.

"Happy Birthday" is belted out in bad harmony. Even my mom, who has her arm around Beth, is singing loudly. The tiny room is so full of happy off-key noise, I almost don't hear the doorbell ring.

There are five plates, five people. There is no one missing.

I am stuck in birthday cake prison — my gut pressed into the table, the back of my chair scraping our cabinets. Katherine, who is off to the side, grabs my camera from the table and bails midsong into the living room to answer the door.

Suddenly, I'm five years old. I don't want her touching my present.

The doorbell rings again.

Is that Davey? I mouth to Maria. Maybe a ring-and-run to protest his exclusion from our guest list? She shrugs.

Beth keeps smiling, and drags out the *youuuuuuu* as long as her lungs will let her.

My birthday candles flicker, begging to be wished upon. I take a deep breath, but get distracted by a flash of white light in the living room.

Katherine bounds back into the kitchen and flicks a freshly snapped Polaroid at me like a Frisbee. "Someone's here for you."

Blurry features slowly sharpen in my hands. But I only need to see the gap teeth develop before I know who's here.

My dad.

A tall, lean man steps forward and fills the door frame, an unlit cigar stub clenched between his teeth. He holds some pink flowers down at his side. They are carnations, I think. The bunch is wrapped up in clear plastic and secured with a dirty red rubber band, like the bouquets you can buy at the gas station or 7-Eleven when you haven't planned far enough ahead to go to a real florist.

He clears his throat with a thick guttural cough and his eyes lock onto my birthday cake. "Happy birthday, Rubes," he says, but doesn't look at me.

"Thank you," I whisper and scratch a hardened piece of mozzarella off the table.

I used to obsess about what I might say to my dad if I ever saw him again. Not for the last several years, but when I was a kid and things were really messy. I even wrote a never-to-be-delivered letter when I was ten, at the request of the school guidance counselor, who thought it would help my *issues*. It was four pages long, written front and back on bright pink construction paper. I can't remember much of what was in it, and I'll never know for sure because Beth and I microwaved the stupid letter until it caught fire so I wouldn't have to find it again and have it upset me. But I am so totally positive I never, ever wrote *thank you*.

Mom flicks on the light and everything is too bright and too real. I blink a few times, half expecting my dad to disappear.

"Jim," she says in the same surprised voice reserved for when you run into a neighbor at the supermarket. I wince, hating that there's even a hint of friendliness in her voice. "You should have called. You . . ." Her face fights both smiles and frowns as she struggles to finish her sentence. There are too many options.

His grip tightens around the flowers and crackles the cellophane. "Yeah. I thought about that." Still in the doorway, he shifts his weight from dirty work boot to dirtier work boot. He's afraid to enter the kitchen, and it's too late to run.

All these long-buried feelings are rising up and churning around, but, thankfully, I can't seem to hold on to a single painful thought.

Maria's lips move silently at Katherine: *I think that's her dad.*

"Who?" Katherine blurts out. Maria slaps her hand over Katherine's mouth.

"I wanted to get you a dozen," Dad says, ignoring my friends and sheepishly extending the bouquet in my direction. He doesn't explain why there are only six.

Beth takes a step back from the table, like the whole scene is too intense for her to be standing so close. We lock eyes for a moment and I silently beg her to tell me what I'm supposed to do. She's always been the one with all the answers, ready to help me through any tough time I might be having. And I need her now, more than ever before. But her face is frozen. She's not even blinking.

Dad's eyes finally settle on my face. Everyone is looking at me now. They all wait patiently for me to give them a cue. To see if this surprise family reunion might be my birthday wish come true. But my candles are still lit and, thankfully, I can't even remember the last time I saw him. So I make a wish to keep on forgetting and blow them out.

"Rubes," he says again. The bouquet sinks slightly. "These are for you." His voice drips with expectancy. Like I owe him something. It's almost funny. But I don't want to laugh. I want to scream.

"THANK YOU!" I shriek at the top of my lungs, suddenly springing to life. My chair leg catches on a buckle in the floor, and I hip check the table to allow for my escape. Droplets of melted wax and ice cream splatter all across the pictures I've taken.

Someone gasps. Maybe everyone does. The volume of my voice even freaks me out. These are the only two words I can think of, so I repeat them over and over. "THANK YOU, THANK YOU, THANK YOU," as loud as I possibly can, between gulps of air. Each word coincides with a room-shaking stomp as I stalk around the kitchen table until my dad and I are face-to-face.

Measured against him, it hits me how tall I am. And I see more of myself in his face than the gap between my teeth. The steep slant of his nose, the pale green of his eyes, a ridiculously pouty lower lip. I don't want to notice these things. I don't want to be like him at all.

I snatch the flowers out of his hand. A few stems break, some petals fall. We are nearly chin-to-chin. The only air I can inhale is what pours out of his partially open mouth. It smells peppery, like his cigars. It's so potent, like he's breathing clouds into my face.

We lock eyes and I don't dare blink. I want to make him sorry that he's come here.

He wipes his watery eyes with the sleeve of his flannel coat. He is just sorry.

I drop the bouquet and run out of the room.

"Ruby!" Mom calls after me.

Outside, the cold October air pricks my hot cheeks like a thousand tiny needles. My body throbs equal parts adrenaline and embarrassment. For a moment, I don't know where to go. What I should do.

The front door opens behind me. I turn around and see Maria emerging from my house, keys in hand. Beth comes next, holding my sweatshirt. Katherine pushes past her. I allow myself the smallest sigh of relief. We dive into Maria's ancient orange Volvo while she turns her key a few times, pounding her foot on the clutch.

An old blue pickup truck blocks us in the driveway. As soon as the engine catches, Maria guns her car onto my front lawn and pulls around it, carving tracks into the dying grass and cakey soil. We jump the curb and the spinning tires squeal against the asphalt.

Maria's hands strangle the steering wheel. "Oh my God! You scared the living crap out of him!"

"Screw that. You scared the living crap out of *me*," Katherine mumbles, fumbling for a cigarette.

Maria checks her rearview mirror. It's strangled with a hundred of those sickly sweet yellow air freshener trees, swishing violently from side to side. "I don't think he's following us," she says, taking a turn way too fast. She slows down and allows a deep breath. "That was insane!"

I shiver off the goose bumps popping up on my bare arms. I don't know what to say, so I press my lips together and concentrate on breathing.

Beth wraps my sweatshirt around my shoulders. "I've been waiting for you to have a moment like that for six years, ever since the day your dad left."

Then it hits me. It's over. I finally have closure — the best birthday present I could have asked for. The murkiness of my mind gives way to one clear, honest feeling that I don't try to hide from.

I want to celebrate.

TWO

Maria makes a left onto Copley Road, Akron's main drag. We drive for a few minutes until a three-story-high neon bowling pin sprouts out of the ground. We're approaching Akron Pinz and I'm ready to salvage what little time is left on my birthday clock. I honestly don't care about anything else.

Akron Pinz is a notorious weekend hangout. It has a huge parking lot, which is key for scoping out who might be there at any given time. It's also a total dive, with few patrons to hassle us or, worse, report our antics. Best of all, the bowling alley is butted up against a large and dense park, which provides lots of natural camouflage.

The place is totally deserted tonight, except for a couple of cars cuddled together underneath the single spotlight illuminating the lot. We pull past them and come to a stop at the very edge of the park, near a small wood-chip-strewn playground erected in honor of a little kid who died of cancer two years ago. You can always find flowers tied up to the chain-link fence. I usually try not to look at them, because it's totally depressing.

But tonight, they momentarily steal my attention away from the impending birthday fun. They're just like the ones my dad brought for me, except white.

Beth and I kick out on two creaky rubber swings, while Katherine climbs on top of the monkey bars. Maria flops onto a bench across from us, her face fuzzy in the darkness. A glimpse of purple satin underwear peeks out from her jean skirt.

"So what am I in store for tonight?" I ask Maria, pointing at the stuffed knapsack next to her. It's partially unzipped and a few plastic bags are popping out. "Are we partying it up Dollar Store style?" I'm sure I sound suspiciously cheery.

Maria hesitates and pulls the knapsack onto her lap, like she's not sure if it's okay to ignore what just happened back at my house, now that the adrenaline's worn off. But Beth leaps up from her swing, races to Maria's side, and gives her a little nudge. With Beth's blessing, Maria suddenly can't fight the smirk tugging at the corner of her mouth. She unzips the bag and pulls out an opaque green bottle of champagne. A dozen curly pink ribbon strings are wrapped around the neck.

"Whoa! Where'd you get that?" I've never really drunk before, except for the couple of dented cans of warm beer we smuggled out of Beth's garage at her family's last Fourth of July barbecue. Never something as fancy as this.

"Nothing's too good for your Sweet Sixteen!" Beth commandeers the bottle, her tiny hands cradling the neck. The cork pops off and sails into the darkness. "And you better remember that next week, when it's *my* birthday."

Katherine grabs the bottle from her and presents it to me with some grand game-show hand gestures that make everyone laugh, even me. "Seriously though, my mom's boss sent it to her for helping him on the weekend with some report. Lucky for us, I was the only one home when the delivery guy showed up."

"Isn't that cool?" Beth says, jumping up and down behind Katherine. "We should totally do this kind of stuff more often!"

I spend a second translating the label before I remember that I barely passed French my freshman year. I take a deep, celebratory sip. The crisp, appley bubbles swill and expand in my mouth, more than I expect them to. Some overflow dribbles down the front of my white T-shirt.

"Nice one," Katherine snarks, shielding a freshly lit match from the wind with cupped hands.

I am ordered to sit and drink while my friends set up a total old-school park birthday party, the kind little kids have in the springtime. My mind tries to wander back to my house, to think about what might be going on there between my mom and dad, but I don't let it. Instead, I lock onto the details around me. Maria hangs streamers from low branches. Katherine strings up a star-shaped piñata from the monkey bars. Beth duct-tapes Pin the Tail on the Donkey to a big gnarly oak. I wish I hadn't left my camera at home. I want to make sure this is what I remember about tonight.

"I can't believe you guys went to all this trouble for me," I say, taking another sip. The bottle is nearly half empty. I guess I should slow down.

"I can't believe you still feel like celebrating," Maria says in a quiet voice, and chucks a roll of streamers over a low branch. "Not like I know the history or anything, but what was that all about?"

"No clue," I say, and pull my arms inside my sweatshirt.

Beth rips off a piece of duct tape with gritted teeth. "All guys are the same. It's like they've got special radar and, when they sense you're completely over them, they show up again just for the sake of messing with your head." She pauses to take a sip from my bottle. "Pete Southern did the same thing about a month after he dumped me. But it was beyond too late for any apologies. Right, Ruby?"

Pete was Beth's first and only boyfriend. They dated for about two months last year and their unexpected breakup was really hard on her. I guess there are a few similarities. The tip of my nose feels icy, so I pull my head down into my T-shirt like a turtle to warm it up. I can make out Beth's shape through the thin cotton.

She takes a step toward me. "Ruby, you know there isn't an *I'm sorry* big enough in the entire world to ever make up for how he bailed on you and your mom."

It's true. My dad is a total loser and not at all worth any of my waning birthday hours. But I don't want to start some big discussion about this. I pop my head out and walk back over to sit down on a swing.

"It just seems so random," Maria says. "I think — "

Beth interrupts her with a heavy sigh. "Listen, the worst thing we could do is let him ruin Ruby's birthday."

"I totally agree," I say, pumping my legs and picking up some speed. "It's a nonissue. It's over. So let's quit talking about it, okay?"

Katherine picks a scab off her elbow. "Why'd your dad leave in the first place?"

Beth sticks her finger up in the air. "Okay. Wait up. If we're going to talk about this, no one can refer to *him* as Ruby's dad. Because he's *not*. He's essentially a stranger."

It's weird to hear someone say that about your dad. But Beth's right. He hasn't been that for a long, long time, and I've got to keep reminding myself of it.

Katherine rolls her eyes. "Well, what should we call him then? What's his name?"

"It's Jim," I say.

"Fine. Then why'd *Jim* leave in the first place?"

Maria's head perks up.

There's no way to hide the pissy tone in my voice, so I don't even try. "I don't know, Katherine. I guess he fell out of love with my mom." What a stupid question.

"He doesn't pay child support, does he?" Maria drags a stick through the dirt.

"Not really." I think we used to get money orders every so often. But not for a long time. That's why Mom is always at the hospital, picking up extra shifts.

"Maybe this will help your mom finally move on." Maria crosses, then uncrosses her legs. "'Cause, I mean, she's totally hot. And she doesn't ever date. Right?"

The party scene whirls past my eyes as I swing higher and higher. "Right. She doesn't." I make my voice sound as flat as possible, so Maria and Katherine will get the hint already and remember that this is my party, not a therapy session. Maria shoots me an apologetic smile and returns to streamer duty.

For a second, I feel bad. I know Maria has a lot of questions about my family situation. Maybe it's weird that we've never really talked about it before, even though I consider her a close friend. The thing is, I don't have any details to give. Dad left, Mom's heart was broken, she completely shut down, and I went a little bit crazy dealing with everything on my own. But I eventually learned how to handle it, with Beth's help. The whole story ended tonight with me walking out that door. The beginning doesn't matter anymore.

My swing creaks back, blowing my hair across my face. At the apex, Katherine materializes dead center before me. I rush forward and grind the toes of my Converses into the wood chips to keep myself from plowing into her. The world catches up to me in three-second swirling delay.

I'm pretty tipsy.

Katherine's forehead creases with deep thought. "But what about you, Ruby?"

I use my sneaker to smooth the splayed wood chips around me. My hands feel clammy around the cool metal chains. "What about me?"

"He fell out of love with your mom. I get that. But why'd your dad leave *you*?"

Katherine might as well have kicked me in the chest. I can't seem to catch my breath.

"Not cool, Katherine," Maria says, and rolls her eyes.

"Seriously," Beth says.

Katherine puffs up. "What? That's a valid question! Lots of people get divorced, but still stay close to their kids. I mean, that's why my dad's getting an apartment across town."

Beth runs over and stands next to me. "Katherine, your situation is completely — " she begins, but then her cell phone rings. She fishes it out of her pocket and holds the screen up to my face.

My home number.

I shake my head, unable to push words out of my mouth. She hands the phone to Maria, who answers it and drifts away toward the fence.

"Listen. None of this is about Ruby," Beth says. "Jim's having some stupid midlife crisis. He's trying to make himself feel better so he can go on with his life somewhere else."

"Sure," Katherine says quietly, before tipping her head back and taking a huge sip of champagne. "I guess that could be it."

"That *is* it," Beth insists. "And the best part is that Ruby didn't let him off the hook." She pats me on the back. "Tonight was the best thing that could have happened for you, Ruby. Trust me."

Maria returns, pushing aside a clump of dangling streamers. She forces a smile.

"What did her mom say?" Beth asks.

"She wanted to make sure Ruby is okay. And that we'd have her home by midnight. She sounded totally normal. Not crying or anything."

I'm not surprised. Mom doesn't cry in front of me. She's definitely not going to be all blubbery to Maria. Still, seeing Dad had to be hard for her. "Was he there?" I ask, suddenly finding my voice. Because seeing him leave us again would be even worse.

Beth cocks her head to the side. "Do you want him to be there?"

Something about the way Beth asks this question makes me think it's a trick. I feel like the answer tattooed on my heart is *maybe*. Or maybe even *yes*. But I focus on the good-for-me answer, the one my brain is screaming, the one I know is right. "No. I don't."

Beth rewards me with a hug.

"Well, she didn't say either way," Maria tells me. Then she adds, "Sorry, Ruby. I should have asked her that."

I guess I look pretty pathetic, all glum and hunched over, clinging to the swing like a little kid. Beth steps on the toes of my sneakers. She takes my hands and shakes out my arms. Then, tipping her weight back, she pulls me up off the swing. "I'd be a pretty terrible friend if we didn't have some fun tonight. So let's get to it already and put all this behind you for good."

We make the best of our final hour. We freeze-dance in the headlights while Katherine mans the car stereo. We prank everyone in Maria's phone. Gifts are given. Beth has knitted me a skinny, gray wool scarf with butter-yellow ribbons laced through the stitches. It's instantly the prettiest thing I own. Maria has bought me an old Cooper Rubber T-shirt from Revival, our town's vintage resale store. Katherine is presentless, but writes me an IOU for a CD of my choice on a napkin she finds in the Volvo's glove compartment. After the last few sips of my champagne, I cheat at Pin the Tail on the Donkey, but lose anyway. Everyone takes a swing at the piñata with a splintered tree branch. Katherine finally cracks it with a tire iron she finds in Maria's trunk. We wrestle on the ground for the candy necklaces, plastic bracelets, and super bouncy rubber balls that rain down.

I use up the last of my energy to convince myself that I am actually having a good time. If for nothing more than to spite him. Then I spend most of the ride home semi-passed out against the passenger-side window, my forehead sticking to the glass. I can hear the conversations around me, but I can't muster the energy to participate.

"Did you like your champagne, birthday girl?" Maria rustles my hair, and it feels like a tornado across my scalp.

"A little too much, I think," Beth says, smoothing my bangs and securing them off my face with one of her bobby pins.

"I love you guys," I mumble.

"That's just the liquor talking," Maria jests.

"Here, take this." The strong scent of mint tickles my nose. I open my bleary eyes and Katherine hands me a mouthwash strip sandwiched between two pieces of gum. "Your mom won't smell anything on your breath but spearminty freshness. Trust me, it works every time."

Though it takes a lot of effort, I manage to thank her.

The Volvo shuffles over a wide set of train tracks and we've arrived at my street. A respectful silence blankets us as everyone looks at my house. I cover my eyes with my hand but end up peeking through my fingers. The house is dark, the driveway is empty.

Before they say good-bye, all of the girls invite me to sleep over in case I don't want to go home. I turn them down with a barrage of mumbled and embarrassed thank-yous because I've got nothing to run from.

I use the spare key hidden over the porch awning to enter the house. The television in my mom's bedroom softens. She doesn't want to talk, only to know that I am home safe. I do her the favor of helping myself to the noisiest glass of water imaginable.

Tonight's Polaroids are in a stack next to an ashtray in the kitchen. There is only one cigar butt mashed inside, but the entire room reeks like a chimney. I empty the ashtray and think about throwing away the pictures too, knowing the one of Jim is shuffled somewhere in the pile. But I decide against it and hide them in the silverware drawer, in case tonight is really the last time I ever see him.

The thought of that, or maybe the smell of smoke, brings tears to my eyes.

I crack the window before heading up to bed, because I definitely don't want to smell this in the morning.

THREE

His leaving seemed sudden at the time.

I was on the living room floor in my sleeping bag, hair divided into two still-damp pigtails, trying to watch *Annie* for the millionth time. I say *trying*, because Dad walked past the screen like every five seconds and ruined all the best dance numbers. Back and forth and back and forth and back and forth. When I was annoyed enough to make a fuss, I found him snatching the last of his dusty records from the shelf.

This instantly struck me as strange behavior because the records were ancient and I had never heard them played. In fact, we didn't even own a record player. So I crept behind him toward the master bedroom to investigate.

Mom had wedged herself into the tiny space between the nightstand and her dresser. Her back was up against the wall like a criminal in an alleyway — completely out of Dad's way.

We watched Dad cram the last of his possessions into an overstuffed trash bag. Two large suitcases had already been filled and waited in the doorway. Mom wasn't crying or making a

26

scene. She just stood stiff as a statue with her hands folded over her nursing scrubs. She didn't even acknowledge me when our eyes met for a brief second.

Even though it was already dark and the middle of winter, I ran outside without stopping for a jacket. My bare feet crunched in the iced-over snow that no one had shoveled from that afternoon's storm. I leapt up on the hood of that blue truck and sat with my back against the frosty windshield. Brisk cold seeped through my gauzy pajamas. I shivered and shook, but there was no way I was going to move. I had to stop him from leaving.

Snow crunched helplessly under his work boots. Dad dropped his things in the bed of his truck. He told me twice to get down, but I didn't listen. Hot tears streamed off my cheeks.

When he looped his arms under my armpits and lifted me off the hood, I arched my back and let my limbs hang like dead weight. It was a game we used to play when I was little. But instead of tickling me or groaning in fake struggle, my dad set me off to the side of the driveway like it was nothing. And, without a word, he got in his blue truck and drove away.

FOUR

The salty smell of breakfast seeps underneath my comforter, where I am buried, eyes squinted shut. Bright sun radiates heat and light through the bedding and bakes me like pie filling.

But I shiver, as if I were still freezing cold, still out on the hood of his truck. I haven't thought of the day he left in years, but suddenly I'm reliving it in such sharp detail that it takes my breath away. It's not like a dream or a flashback, where things seem all soft and muddy and confused. This is different. This feels as real and painful as it did the first time. I brush away a clump of damp hair from my face and kick the covers off.

Mom stands at the foot of my bed in her mint-green nursing scrubs, staring down at me. The skin around her eyes is dark and puffy, even though she's put makeup on to try and hide it. She probably hasn't slept a wink. I doubt I would have either, if not for passing out cold on my pillow after praying that I wouldn't throw up. I'm never, ever drinking again.

She's holding a plate piled high with scrambled eggs, toast, and a neat stack of bacon. A huge glass of water and an economy-sized bottle of Advil are wedged in the crook of her arm. I can't remember the last time she cooked me breakfast, though I doubt my brain is really working properly. It feels like it hates me, the way it pounds and amplifies the steady beat of Mom's slipper tapping the carpet to a frighteningly loud decibel level.

"You slept right through your alarm this morning. I had to come in here and shut it off myself."

"Sorry," I say, reaching for the water with the Advil. My tongue feels like a dried orange peel as it presses two tablets against the scaly roof of my mouth. I start gulping.

Mom shifts her weight from left to right. Her shiny hair flips shoulders accordingly. "I let school know you wouldn't be in today, seeing as it's nearly two P.M."

The red dots on my digital clock look blurry and fat through the bottom of the glass. Every part of me feels heavy, sinking deep into the grooves worn into my old mattress, but I can't get comfortable. Mom clears some junk from my nightstand and sets the plate down. I keep swallowing until the glass is empty, and then trade it for a fork she's got stuffed in her pocket.

"Is it safe for your mother to assume that coming home drunk will not be behavior she can expect from you on a regular basis?" Slipping into third person is Mom's trademark of being annoyed, another way to put more distance between us.

Sharp pain ripples across my forehead, but I force myself to nod through it.

"Good answer. Then suffering through your first hangover will be your only punishment. You can consider this Get Out of Jail Free card a belated birthday present. But know that if you ever come home intoxicated again, you'll be grounded like

29

there's no tomorrow." She plants her hands on her hips and waits for me to formally acknowledge the huge amount of parental slack I've just been granted.

So I mumble, "Umm . . . thank you."

A smirk creeps across her mouth. "That was quite a tirade last night. At least your father knows I've raised one *very polite* teenager."

This is how my mom and I communicate. Sarcasm acts like smoke and mirrors, so we can talk about something without having to actually say anything. But her punch line lights the fuse of my memory. I see flashes of faces gawking at me by birthday candlelight, feel sparks of soreness in my throat from my courteous rant, hear the crackle of cellophane in his tightening fist. He was here, but now he's gone. Again.

"First off, he's *not* my father." I half expect her to defend him, but she doesn't say anything. "And what did he want me to say? *'Hello there! Umm . . . gee, this is awkward, but what's your name again? Ahh, that's right . . . Dad! I totally didn't recognize you there! Would you care for some cake?'*" A clump of eggs slides off my quivering fork. I might still be a little bit drunk.

Mom walks over to my window and opens it wide. I'm glad, because her perfume is thick in the hot room and my first bite of breakfast tastes like a mouthful of overripe petals. Sharp October wind pours in and tangos with the heat of my radiator. She stands there quietly for a minute, peering down at the front lawn.

While her back is turned, she says, "I don't know what he expected and I'm certainly not going to guess. But it's obvious what he wanted. He wanted to see you."

Her words get colder the longer they hang in the air. Maybe she's jealous, because she's the one who actually still seems to care about him. At least I have a best friend who's helped me deal with everything. My mom has nothing but work and awkward conversations with me.

"Well, he got what he wanted," I say through squishy bites of buttery toast. "Now he can go on back to wherever he's been hiding for another six years, because we don't need him."

She turns back around to face me, and we wrestle our lips into weak smiles. Then she pulls out the dirty towels from my hamper while I eat, and both of us ignore the uncomfortable silence that has settled over my room. Just like always. It's almost comforting.

Mom flips the hamper lid shut and makes for the door. My throat suddenly feels tight and I swallow hard to force shards of bacon down. Something triggers my gag reflex. But it's not food that bubbles up.

"So, did he say anything to you last night? Like . . . where he's been for the last six years?" My voice is tinny and high-pitched. It doesn't sound anything like me.

Mom surveys the distance left between her and my open bedroom door. Her shoulders slump and her lungs empty with one deep sigh. "Yeah. He did."

I sit up too fast and my bloated gut seizes in protest, swishing around remains of last night's champagne. Mom sits down on my comforter. Her bottom lip catches under the ridge of her front teeth. I wait patiently and avoid eye contact.

"Your dad's been living in Oregon."

"Oregon?"

"Yes. At least, until last week." Her voice stays even and measured. "Apparently, he was a park ranger there."

I look for an edge to these two puzzle pieces. Some kind of cheat to link *park ranger* and *Oregon* with what little I know

31

about Jim. But they are blobs from somewhere in the hazy, undeveloped middle of What Happened. I have no idea where or how they belong. Or why I even care.

A few seconds pass before my breathing kick-starts. "A park ranger? In Oregon?"

She bites at her pinky nail.

"Mom."

"Ruby." She matches my tone exactly. Then her head dips back and rolls around her shoulders a full 360 degrees. "Okay, fine." She sounds tired and annoyed. Not with the conversation. With me. I grip two fistfuls of my comforter and let her continue. "After you left, he sat down and asked if he could smoke."

My nostrils flare. "You should have told him no."

"I honestly didn't know what to do. His hands were so shaky; it took him about half a book of broken matches before he got one lit. It was very awkward and very quiet, so I got the dustpan out and swept up your flowers. But I did ask him what he's been doing these days. He said he's been living in Oregon, working as a park ranger, but now he's moving on to something new." Her fluttering lashes mask her eyes. "And he said, 'Tell Rubes I'm real sorry for ruining her party.' Then he left."

Cold sweat beads on my temples. "That's it?" That can't be it.

"Don't look so surprised. You should know by now that your dad isn't particularly good at apologies." She couches it in a hollow chuckle, because she's not being mean. Just honest.

I cram the million other questions I have back down my throat.

Mom shakes out her arm until a gold watch slides to her wrist. She checks the time and says matter-of-factly that she better get over to the hospital, as if our conversation needed an official ending. Leaning over, she takes a bite of the toast in my hand and plants a quick kiss on my cheek. Her gooey lipstick deposits sticky crumbs on my face.

"Sorry," she says. And she wipes my face clean.

I don't bother to clarify the intention of her apology.

On her way out of the room, she bends over to pick something up off my floor. "Oh, Ruby. This is beautiful!" She rubs my gray birthday scarf against the side of her face.

"Yeah. Beth made it for me."

Her fingers trace the yellow ribbons. "She's such a good friend." Mom carefully folds the scarf up and lays it on top of my dresser, making me feel crappy that it was ever on the floor in the first place.

I roll away from the rest of my breakfast and fill my face with the pillow until her car scuttles down the driveway. Then our tiny house is quiet, except for the silence, which seems extraordinarily loud. There's no sleeping through this kind of silence. So I get up and take a shower.

My fingers jerk hard and fast through soapy knots of hair. I squint my eyes so tight while I rinse that, when I open them again, the colored spots take forever to fade from the white bathroom tile. Not once but twice, the bar of Ivory flies out of my hands. Every movement feels clumsy and awkward. So I make the executive decision not to shave my legs, even though they're pretty prickly.

It's certainly no secret that I've got some serious emotional baggage. Make that a complete set of luggage with wheels for easy transportation, zippered sections for compartmentalizing, and ballistic nylon for an impenetrable shell. But I remind myself that there's no need to worry. All my issues are packed nicely and neatly away. Just because Jim randomly showed up doesn't mean I have to relive everything all over again. Once was more than enough.

The water turns icy and my skin is pruned. I run to my freezing room and slam the window shut. I squeegee myself with a towel and pull up my favorite Levi's. They feel chalky and in desperate need of a wash, just the way I like them. I shiver into a white tank top and a Japanese Coca-Cola T-shirt I found at Revival, twist a pile of my thick wet hair on top of my head, and secure it with a rubber band. I take one more Advil and start a load of towels in the washing machine.

Then I crash onto our puffy floral couch. The late afternoon light makes everything in the living room look dusty. Traces of leftover cigar smoke burn through my nose.

I try not to think of Oregon. Oregon. Oregon.

Especially because it's a very boring train of thought. I don't know a thing about the state, other than its general Pacific Northwestness.

The Internet might enlighten me a bit, if not for our hulking paperweight of a computer. Wedged in the corner of the room, it's covered in catalogs, credit card offers, and receipts. The sickly green monitor is practically bigger than our television set and the dial-up modem can barely handle a heated IM discussion. We can't afford a new computer, but we might as well throw this one out. It's completely useless.

Then I remember. My map.

It hung on my bedroom wall in our old house — a temporary cosmetic concealer for the garish metallic wallpaper Jim promised he'd strip and replace with something nicer when he had a chance. Each state was a different pastel color. I'm almost positive that Oregon was pale yellow. That's a pretty weird thing to remember. But my post-shower chill is suddenly replaced by a shade of warmth.

I head up the creaky attic stairs, past the bulk toilet tissue and paper towels we buy from Costco. I throw all my weight into the door to get it open. Inside the main room, packed moving boxes are bricked tall like the Great Wall of China.

We used to live in the smallest of the Victorian homes on Rose Lane, but it was still enormous by anyone's standards. My parents bought it cheap because it was classified as a Fixer-Upper — meaning it had been left vacant and uncared for after the bulk of the Akron rubber industry shifted overseas.

Tiny flecks of white house paint would flutter in the air like confetti whenever it got windy. Roof tiles wriggled loose and got lost in the tall grass of the front yard. The pipes leaked and made patches of ceiling turn rusty. Some of the rooms had exposed nails poking through the raw studs, which I was warned to be careful around. It was creaky, run-down, and pretty spooky, especially at night. But the house was also full of endearingly weird quirks, like false-bottom floorboards, sliding doors that would disappear into the wall, and a hidden back staircase that Beth and I filled with stuffed animals and made into a hideout.

I loved that house. I'd never forget that house.

Mom and Jim had planned to restore it together. A labor of love. But up until the time he left, most of their repair projects were in various states of half-ass. The perfect metaphor for their relationship, I guess. Mom pledged to finish the place herself, but that never happened. Partly because he took all his tools with him. Though I seriously doubt she could have done that kind of work alone anyhow.

Two years later, property taxes went up in our neighborhood. Mom and I moved to a tiny two-bedroom row house across Akron that was practically the size of an apartment. We packed up the old house together. At that time, I had been doing okay for a few months. My grades had gone back up and I had stopped seeing the school counselor. But moving shattered any progress I might have made. I think I cried the entire time. It was like I was being forced to look at all these things from my old life and then bury them in boxes forever. It must have been unbearable for Mom. But the one pacifier to the whole situation, which Mom made sure to constantly remind me of, was that our new house was just around the corner from Beth's.

I restack a few of the boxes off to the side to gain access to a cardboard poster tube in the corner. The plastic cap makes a hollow pop that echoes through the room.

The map is not nearly as big as I remember it to be, stretching barely the length of my arm. Random boxes make for an uneven display surface, so I unfurl only the top left corner and press it against a stack at eye level. The rest of the map uncoils sloppily off to the side. A slight tear grows through a state that may or may not be Wyoming.

Well, I was right. Oregon is yellow. Ohio is blue.

But beyond that, there's no real information about the state except for its capital, Salem, a couple of brown triangles indicating the Cascade Mountain Range, and a tiny cartoon horse with a cowboy on top. I squint forward, as if something secret might suddenly emerge if I just stare hard enough, long enough.

Then I spot it. A fleck at the peak of the cowboy's hat. It looks like a pinprick. It looks like his plan to leave us.

Another wave of nausea crashes over me and I get clammy. My hand shakes as I carefully reach forward, as if I were adjusting one of the logs in a campfire.

But the fleck sticks to my damp fingertip. It's dust. It's nothing at all.

A plastic tarp rustles and I jump. My sweaty bare feet slip on the attic floor and I fall hard into one of the boxes. A corrugated corner jabs my pathetically untoned bicep. I touch the red spot softly and find it's already tender and lumpy, a definite bruise in the making. Across the room, the tarp flutters again. From the ground, I can see it's draped over a hissing heat vent.

I pull my knees up to my chin and wonder what it is that I'm doing up here in the first place, and what kind of grand revelation I expect from a stupid third-grade classroom map.

FIVE

I fight through gusts of fall wind, the tails of my scarf flapping wildly behind me. I sink my face into the folds until my eyelashes bat away woolly strands. Autumn has peaked, and the trees are on fire with color.

As I wait for a stoplight to change, I find myself underneath one insanely bright orange-leafed tree. I stare up at the netting of delicate branches splayed overhead like the inside of an umbrella. It's chokingly beautiful.

So I take out my camera from my bag and snap my first real picture. Maybe I could make a collection, like flashcards of beautiful things that I could look at whenever I'm feeling down. Or maybe that's dumb. I doubt the pictures could ever look as good as the real thing. Especially Polaroids. As cool as they are, they always seem a little bit out of focus.

The sidewalks are mostly deserted, save for random old ladies shuffling along with carts commandeered from the Giant Eagle parking lot, or smiling young moms pushing strollers and chatting into their hands-free cell-phone wires. After a few minutes of brisk walking without any real game plan, I'm on the main drag of tiny mom-and-pop stores on West Market that have somehow survived all the strip-mall development.

The temperature is pretty chilly, so I zip up my navy-blue hooded sweatshirt and cram my hands into the shallow pockets. The flashing bank clock across the street says it's almost three. Since Akron High School is about as far away as my house at this point, I decide to head over in that direction and meet up with Beth and the girls. It's weird, but it feels like forever since I've seen them.

Akron High is your typical brick fortress, surrounded by usually green, but now crispy brown, lawns. I can see students inside three floors of classrooms. The parking lot off to the side displays the vast spread of wealth in town — boxy maroon four-doors from the mid-90s reflect in the polished chrome rims of the sleek silver imports parked next to them. Company allegiance is printed in the white letters circling each tire. Firestone and Cooper and the local favorite, Goodyear.

I walk up and down each row until I find Maria's orange Volvo, Goodyear tires. The car is pretty beat up, with dents and dings in the metal and rips in the beige interior, but it always gets us where we need to go. The funniest thing is the back left seat, which we all call the Period Seat. Once Maria tossed a lipstick over her shoulder and it melted in the summer heat and stained the cloth just like a period. It went unused after that, but now that there are four of us, someone always has to sit in the Period Seat. We take turns, rotating around from shotgun. Beth always jokes how just sitting in that seat gives her cramps.

I jump up on the hood and wait until the sound of the final bell catches on a cool breeze. When it does, Maria is the first to walk out. She sees me and blows me kisses with both of her mitten-covered hands. Beth is right behind her. She has on a pair of brown wide-leg polyester pants, stolen out of her granny's suitcase when she last came to visit. Her pace quickens when she spots me, and the fabric bells swish wildly around her ankles. She comes up nose-to-nose with me and grabs the strings on my sweatshirt. One hard yank and the hood shrinks until only my lips are exposed.

"Where were you? I must have called your house a thousand times!" She sounds pretty pissed. And worried. "Are you okay?"

I hop off the hood and stretch my arms like a worn veteran of many drunken nights out. "Mom let me ride out my hangover in bed. She even delivered me a full breakfast. Eggs and toast and all that."

Beth rolls her eyes, still semi-annoyed at me but happy to see that I'm doing all right after last night. She shrugs off her book bag, which I hold while she puts on her jean jacket. Rain clouds swarm overhead in remarkably fast motion.

"Weird! So she wasn't pissed?" Maria walks around to the back of her car, pops the trunk open, and carelessly tosses her books inside one by one.

"Nah. She gave me a No Drinking Lecture, but I'm not grounded or anything." The truth is, I bet my mom was just happy that I came home in one piece. The power of pity is an amazing thing. I should remember that.

Maria slams the trunk closed and cozies up to me against the side door. "Did she get any dirt on your dad? I mean, Jim?" She whispers the last part, almost as if she doesn't want Beth to hear. But she does hear. Her head spins toward us really fast.

I rub the sole of my left sneaker back and forth over the gravel. When I look up, Beth is walking over to us. "It's nothing, trust me," I say.

"Ruby. Spill it." Beth rubs her hands together and blows on them to keep warm.

It's not that I don't want to tell her. More than anything, I'm embarrassed by the whole situation and for what Maria might think about everything. But I ignore the redness burning up my cheeks, unbutton my lips, and recite the two new facts I've learned this morning.

"A forest ranger? You've got to be kidding me," Beth snarls. "Hopefully, karma will strike and a big pine tree will fall on him."

Maria digs in her purse for her favorite lip gloss. She squeezes a dollop on her bottom lip and smoothes it out with her pinky. "Yeah. Tiiiiimber."

Over Beth's shoulder, I spot Katherine trucking across the parking lot with huge athletic strides. Palming an orange basketball, she bobs and weaves around milling students like she's driving for the hoop. The oversized, yellow-mesh uniform hangs comically off her slender frame. Her hair is pulled back into a long, sleek blond ponytail, so tight it yanks up her eyebrows.

She skids to a stop a few feet away from us and shuffles the last few steps. "I waited for you guys at Maria's locker, but you never showed." Her voice is barbed with annoyance. Then she locks eyes with me. "Ruby. I thought you were out sick today."

"I *was* out sick today."

"And we told you to meet us at the car," Beth barks. As sweet as Beth is, she can get pretty snippy when you don't follow the plan. And I can't say that I don't love it when she's snippy with Katherine.

"Oh. Sorry." This time, Katherine's voice is softer. She divides her attention among the three of us and starts over. "Did any of you guys want to come to my basketball game? It should be a good one. There's this girl on the other team that I know from camp and she's got incredible moves underneath the basket. But she can't score on me and it drives her nuts."

"My dad's leaving town tomorrow, so I've got a mandatory dinner," Maria says. I'm secretly jealous that Maria's family has this tradition before his business trips. I imagine the three of them sitting around their dining room, her mom doling out scoops of stuffing and slices of roasted turkey like Thanksgiving. That's just the way it is in my mind, though. Really, her family dinners mean shoes-off sushi on the mini bamboo tables at Little Tokyo. Still. She's lucky. The couples who stay happily married should get some kind of special prize, maybe from the government. Maybe a trophy.

Katherine focuses on me and Beth. "What are you guys up to?" Her nose crinkles up, like she's already sniffing out our crappy excuses.

The truth is that watching a basketball game is about the last thing any of us would want to do, Beth especially. She despises organized athletic activity more than anyone else I know. Last year, she used the asthma excuse so often, Mr. Parisi made her write a ten-page paper on crab soccer to pass gym.

"My mom promised to take me out for another driving lesson." Because Beth's sixteenth birthday is almost a week away, on Halloween, she's as obsessed with getting her license as she is with planning her yearly costume party. I didn't even bother getting mine, because it's not like I'll have a car to drive or any-thing. Mom can barely make ends meet as it is. "But . . . I guess I could get her to take me out after dinner." Then she shoots me a pleading look, like I'm supposed to suffer with her.

It's hard to say no to a friend who has done so much for you. So I quickly run through the positives. I only come up with one — we'll get to hang out alone for a few hours. But that's more than good enough for me, especially with how weird and sentimental I'm feeling. "Yeah, okay. I'll go."

Katherine's face lights up. Even though she can be pretty nasty sometimes, I still feel a flicker of happiness at cracking her surly exterior. She is having a pretty tough time lately. I guess I'm a sucker that way.

Before parting ways, we discuss plans for the evening. Maria is our social director because of all the boys she knows, and she rambles off a list of uninteresting Friday night options, including meeting up with Davey and some of his friends at Pinz. Which I'm kind of over. We've done that for the last three weekends. It's supposed to be really cold out tonight, and I think some of those guys suspect I'm a lesbian because I've never walked hand in hand with them to the dark corners of the park. Not that I have guys throwing themselves at me or anything. I've never even talked to most of them, like one-on-one. I just kind of lurk around other people's conversations and smile or laugh when it's appropriate.

Then Maria says, "Oh, well, I got a random e-mail from Teddy Baker about a party tonight at his house. You guys know him, right?"

Teddy went to grade school with Beth and me, but trans-ferred to Fisher Prep for high school — the sprawling all-boys school next to Akron's golf course. I haven't seen much of him since I was twelve, the year I moved off his block.

"Wait. How do you know Teddy?" I ask.

Maria shrugs. "I hooked up with his friend at a party once, and then he found me online. But a party at Teddy's means lots of boys," she says, waggling her eyebrows. "Lots of richy-rich rubber boys." She sprays the air with machine-gun-style kisses.

"Won't Davey be mad that you're not hanging out with him?" Beth asks.

"Davey's *not* my boyfriend," Maria says. "We haven't even kissed yet."

"Yeah, right," Katherine says.

Maria laughs. "Seriously! Not even one smooch."

"I thought you guys were together," I say.

"Well, we are. Kind of." Maria shakes her head. "We've been hanging out a bunch but it's always more friendly than flirty."

"Seriously?" Beth shakes her head, flabbergasted. "I think it's time for you to move on. You don't want to look desperate, throwing yourself at him if he's not into you."

"Yeah," Maria says, brushing her bangs out of her eyes. "I guess maybe."

We decide to meet at my house to get ready, since my mom will be at work. Maria drives off, sputtering gravel at the backs of our heels as Katherine, Beth, and I make our way toward the gym.

Katherine dribbles her basketball effortlessly through her legs as we walk. "Listen, Ruby," she says, but pauses to clear her throat, spitting a huge yellow ball of smoker's phlegm a few feet ahead of us. "I'm sorry if I came off harsh last night. I'm just going through my own drama. And seeing you freak out on your dad and, like, understanding that all this divorce stuff is going to mess me up for, like, years to come, really made me lose it."

Decoding Katherine's babble is a skill I've yet to master. But I know there's an apology in there somewhere, which is pretty surprising. Until I glance over at Beth, who kicks a bottle cap. The faint smile she wears tells me everything.

"That's okay," I say, opening the double doors for her. And it is. While she might hang out with us, Katherine isn't *really* my friend. I'm not the easiest person to get to get close to, but I keep people like her at a distance for a reason.

Predictably, there are not many people in the gym. Though every inch of wall space is covered by navy-and-yellow felt banners, proclaiming countless championships in every sport imaginable, most are titles won long before I was born. Akron's athletic program has been on the end of a losing season for many many years. The crowd is mostly other basketball players from the freshman and JV girl squads, a few family members, and a bunch of little kids who storm the court at every unoccupied second to shoot free throws or run races to the half-court line and back. We have our pick of uncomfortable bleachers. I follow Beth up to the very top row.

"I'm glad you came," she says, dropping her bag and slumping onto the bench. "After that last fight, no one in Katherine's family would come to cheer for her. It's amazing to me how selfish parents can be." Beth shakes her head dismissively. "She reminds me a lot of you."

"Really?" I say, sliding next to her and trying to hide the disappointment in my voice.

The Akron varsity girls team commandeers the center of the gym for some stretches. Most of the girls are half-assing it, talking and laughing while Katherine calls out counts of ten as sternly as an army drill sergeant. I recognize a few of them from the hallways. Specifically, two tall blondes and a short brunette. They are all wearing lipstick. The brunette catches me staring and points up at me and Beth. The two blondes lean in and all three whisper with curled upper lips, while keeping their eyes locked on us. They are Katherine's old friends.

I pull my sweatshirt over my head to break their gaze.

"Yikes, Ruby! What'd you do?" Beth pokes my arm.

I wince and twist it so I can see the inside of my bicep. There's a deep purple blob, speckled by flecks of red.

My throat fills up with a lump that I force down with a big swallow. "Ugh, this is so stupid. Okay. Well. Do you remember that map I used to have in my bedroom? I don't know why, but I wanted to take a look at Oregon."

Beth blinks a couple of times.

"You know, in my old house. The U.S. map that hid my super ugly wallpaper?"

I search her face for a glimmer of recognition. If anyone should remember something from my life in painstaking detail, it's Beth. But then I realize she's not confused. She knows exactly what I'm talking about.

"Ruby," she says, wrapping my hand inside hers, "I don't think it's such a great idea for you to be thinking like that."

"Like what?"

"Well, like, imagining where Jim might be living or something. Because — and I'm only saying this because I'm your best friend — he's probably not coming back after how things went down last night. And the more you learn about him, the harder he's going to be to forget again." She looks away from me, up at the buzzing lights in metal cages over our head. "You've come so far. Don't let this mess you up."

"I was just curious," I whisper. Though I know she's right. I hardly knew anything about Jim when I was a kid, and it took years for me to get over him leaving. Imagine how tough it would be if he became a real person, instead of a vague idea of what he might really be like.

"I'm just giving you a little friendly advice." She nudges me with her bony shoulder. "That's my job."

The shrill whir of a whistle diverts my attention to the court. Katherine is underneath the basket, wrestling with a girl from the opposing team over a loose ball. Neither wants to let go, so two additional referees add their whistles to the mix. Katherine's throwing crazy elbows, thrashing for control. Finally, the other girl releases her grip, and Katherine screams a hoarse victory cry into her face. The referee blows a final long blast, flashes his hands in the shape of a T, and the angry Akron coach flags Katherine over to the bench.

But Katherine's not quite finished, arguing down the ref and acting like his call was insanely unjustified. The brunette tries to lead her away by the arm, but Katherine flails free and stalks over on her own accord. She crashes onto the bench, grabs a Gatorade bottle, and squeezes a thick green stream down the back of her throat. She spots me in the stands, but doesn't smile.

"Did you see that?" I turn to face Beth, but she's looking at me all googly-eyed.

"Come on," she says and kicks the empty bleacher in front of her. When I don't spring to action she whines, "Ruby! Come on! You know this will make you feel better."

Sometimes, when I'd get really upset about Jim stuff, Beth would sit me on the floor and French braid my hair over and over again until I calmed down. She hasn't had to do it in years, and I'm not even that stressed or anything right now, but I guess she wants me to know she's still there for me, like always. So I slide in front of her and pull out my hair thing. Piles fall down to my shoulders. It still feels damp at my roots from my morning shower.

"Whoa!" she squeals. "Ruby, your hair looks amazing."

"Really?"

She digs frantically in her bag. "Crap. I don't have a mirror. Where's your camera?" Without asking, she digs into my bag and pulls it out. I make a goofy face into the lens, puffing out my cheeks like a chipmunk. Beth snaps the picture and looks pleased. She turns it around. Even though my face looks stupid, my normally flat hair is chunky and wavy, like I've spent the day at the beach. It's almost pretty, which is so not a word I ever use to describe myself.

"Oh, my God! Maybe you and Teddy can finally consummate your marriage tonight."

"What are you talking about?"

She smiles. "You know. A little thing called fourth-grade Halloween, when Teddy was James Bond and you were Princess Diana, marching together in the school parade. Everyone thought you were husband and wife."

We both giggle. It feels really good. "Holy crap. I forgot about that."

"Not at all surprising, considering you have a terribly memory." She rolls her eyes. "Anyhow, I totally predict that you will make out with Teddy tonight." She crosses her arms and nods her head once, like a genie. "It'll be great. You'll kiss all your troubles away."

"Eww!" I say, and stick my tongue out. There's something a little daytime-talk-show about trying not to obsess about your deadbeat dad by randomly hooking up with some guy. Plus, it's not like I have a million other guys I've kissed in my lifetime. There hasn't even been one. And I don't know if I want my first to be tainted with his memory.

"What do you mean *eww*?" Beth pokes a finger at my chest. "Ruby, I'm starting to think that you might have a phobia about hooking up. Like a fear of getting close to a guy or something. Because of your parents."

I actually contemplate her words for a few seconds. But then I notice how Beth's face is super stony and serious. Too serious. "You're so full of it."

She rocks back with laughter. "Then prove me wrong!"

Kissing Teddy might be a good way to take my mind off things. And I don't get many chances to prove Beth wrong about anything. So I flash a crooked grin and decide to seize this particular opportunity by the lips.

SIX

This is going to be a lot harder than I thought.

Admittedly, the idea of distracting myself with a random hookup left me feeling unusually warm and malleable for the rest of Friday. I abandoned all my standard reservations and let Beth take charge of getting me make-out ready. She swept some lilac eye shadow across my lids and pinned back some of my waves with a sparkly barrette. I borrowed Maria's vintage rhinestone earrings and Katherine's wide leather belt. And I even let Beth snip open the collar of my too-old and too-tight Akron Public Library Read-A-Thon T-shirt. Even though I hadn't actually seen Teddy in about four years, I conjured up enough adorable memories of him to get by on for the afternoon, picturing the cute boy who used to take the class hermit crabs home every summer.

The Teddy of tonight, however, is not so much adorable as he is enormous. He's linebacker-huge, with matching tribal bicep tattoos. His neck is easily as thick as my waist, Darwin-mandated to support his big head. Dark rings of perspiration bleed out along the seams of his lime-green polo shirt, a snug extra-extra-large. Droplets twinkle on the sides of his forehead, and when his nervous habit of running his hands through his brown military buzz cut kicks in, sprays of sweat halo his head. There's only one familiar detail — Teddy's still as smiley as ever, especially since his teeth, now freed from the braces of his youth, are perfectly straight and white.

He's being nice and all, but there's no chemistry. Still, I'm trying to remain positive. I'm trying to keep kissing on my mind.

Beth and I have our backs pressed up against the wood panels of Teddy's basement wall. He's standing in front of us, stocky legs spread in an upside-down V, rocking his weight from side to side. I wonder if he knows what's going on, that Beth is baiting him to be my very first kiss.

I'm not talking much, but that's fine because Beth dominates the conversation, OhMyGod!ing so loud and shrill that Teddy's attention can't wander away from us for long. She's retelling the fourth-grade Halloween-parade story. Teddy's mumbling "Yeah, yeah," to be courteous, though his blank stare reveals he has no idea what she's going on about. I don't think Beth picks that up. She's far too busy playing matchmaker, and keeps talking and laughing like the story is the funniest thing ever, a mutual joke among very old and very good friends, a rehearsal of the toast she'll make at our wedding.

In the Budweiser mirror hanging behind us I catch Teddy searching for escape. I suddenly don't feel good.

The muggy room is wall-to-wall with Akron private school elite — boys from Fisher Prep and girls from its sister school, Lambert Academy. For kids who complain about wearing uniforms, everyone's dressed remarkably alike on their off night. Like extras from a television show in California, their clothing is cottony and fitted, in pastel colors that enhance frightening shades of tan for October in Ohio. Girls do their best languid MySpace poses all over each other for flashing camera phones held at arm's length, while the boys pretend not to get boners watching them. It's all totally gross.

Ten o'clock must be too late an arrival for a party with parent-provided liquor, because the crowd is supertrashed. Anyhow, I'm not drinking. Just the smell of beer is making my almost-recovered stomach tempt hangover relapse.

Across the room, some meathead wearing a supertight tank top and an upside-down visor screams about a tapped keg, the ultimate in prep-school party fouls. "I guess I should check that out," Teddy says before quickly ditching us. A cloud of musty cologne lingers in his wake.

"Let's find the girls," I urge Beth. We'd scattered upon entering the party — Maria to make a call, Katherine to get some beer. Beth's number one priority was to get me some face time with Teddy and let the sparks fly. Only they're not flying at all.

Beth hands me her tube of vanilla lip gloss while she adjusts the bobby pins holding her hair off her face. "Teddy's not bad. A little sweaty, but not bad at all. You — " and she knocks me in the shoulder " — should be talking more! You've got to show Teddy you're interested!"

Her dedication to this hookup is my own fault. Beth's happy when I'm happy, and I was definitely happy tonight, tittering over our game plan in the backseat of the Volvo. But now I'm not sure I want my first kiss to be with Teddy, or anybody else here.

My nostrils burn with the scent of a musky hunting lodge, signaling that Teddy's taking another lap around the room.

He trots from partygoer to partygoer, delivering beer, laughing hard at stale jokes, leaping into outstretched arms, and lending his voice to the endless choruses of Holy Shit Dude.

"Seriously, let's mingle a bit," I plead, tugging on Beth's sleeve.

She shakes me off, kind of rough. "Relax, will you?"

I cross one leg in front of the other to keep them both from shaking. This is stupid and embarrassing. It's not like Teddy's even into me. But if Beth wants to pretend like this is going to work out all happy-ending style, far be it from me to ruin her fantasy.

My attention wanders until I spot Mr. Baker jogging down the basement stairs, head nodding to the beat of the music. No one seems the slightest bit alarmed as he snakes his way through the crowd and checks that the two kegs are in perfect working order. He must have heard the ruckus from upstairs.

If it wasn't for his big bald head or his Santa-ish gut, you might mistake Mr. Baker for one of the kids. He's got on a tight white polo shirt and jeans that are conspicuously distressed. They are not Dad Jeans that have faded over time from raking leaves in the yard, oiling up a bicycle chain, or painting a bathroom ceiling. He bought his jeans with Teddy — the very same pair, down to the tiny black skull stitched on the back left pocket. They were probably $200. Each.

Teddy spots his dad and turns bright red. He screams, "Get back upstairs! It's all under control, bro."

Mr. Baker throws up his hands and quickly retreats. He might've even said *chill*, but I really can't hear over the music. Thank God.

"Eww. Did you see that?"

Beth cocks a loaded eyebrow. "How am I supposed to get you kissed with that awful frown you've got plastered on your face?" She twists her body and picks a brown fuzzy off the side of her creamy white sweater. "Don't sabotage this for yourself, Ruby."

My mouth drops open, but before I can defend myself, Teddy walks by us again, cradling four red plastic cups filled to the brim with frothy beer. Beth grabs his arm and pulls him toward us, sending a tidal wave sloshing onto my sneakers. The wetness seeps through to my socks.

"Sorry," Teddy says, but does not slow down, thereby avoiding Beth's trap. He stops a few feet in front of us, distributes the beers, and slides a hand up the short tennis skirt of a girl with twinkling braces, after she loops her arm casually around his shoulders.

I guess he figures it's time to bring Beth up to speed, that he and I were never going to happen. And I can't help but breathe a sigh of relief that we're finally all on the same page.

Unfortunately, Beth doesn't see it quite the same way. "Honestly, Ruby." Her fingers lock into mine and we take off across the crowded room. "Do you even know how to flirt?"

"Yes," I say, dragging my feet. But really, no. But really, it doesn't even matter.

The basement is outfitted with a huge tiki bar, a few arcade games, and vintage corporate signs from Firestone (which, I hate to admit, are actually quite cool). Tiny speakers are nestled in every corner, and hardly one bad song gets played the whole way through before someone commandeers the iPod and click-wheels onto an even worse one. There's a huge flat-screen TV with about five different video game systems lined up on top of the entertainment unit. Glossy posters of waxy bikini girls with sandy crotches

54

are framed and lit like paintings in a museum. The whole basement is officially dubbed a "Dude's Paradise" by a custom-made sizzling blue neon sign. I wonder if it looked like this before Teddy's mom ran away with the dentist. I wonder if that happened before or after his braces came off.

We pass by Katherine, waiting her turn behind three guys at the arcade basketball game, silently chugging from a red cup. She looks really pretty — her blond hair is half up and she has on a tight little black V-neck and jeans. Maria's leaning against the leg of a tall boy draped spread-eagle on the corner of the pool table. I don't want to disturb her flirting, but Beth taps her shoulder and Maria happily breaks away. Only then do I notice the boy has severe acne.

"I can't believe I ever made out with that guy. I asked him what the last CD he bought or downloaded was, and he said he doesn't listen to anything but what's on the radio. Could you be any more boring?" I can't help but think she's comparing him to Davey, but I'm not going to call her out on it. Maria shakes her head, erasing the memory of the bad-skinned boy from her mind like an Etch-a-Sketch. "How're things going with Teddy?"

"Not great," Beth barks before I even get a chance to answer.

The best thing I can do is ignore Beth when she gets pissy. She acted the same way whenever I skated faster than her at the ice rink, or the time I wouldn't ride the log flume with her at Cedar Point because I didn't want to get my clothes wet. So I just smile back at Maria and say, "He's got a girlfriend."

Katherine walks over. "This party sucks," she says in an obnoxiously loud voice, causing a few dirty looks to be sent in our direction. I can't help but laugh, and Maria giggles too.

Beth says, "You guys suck," but in a far less jokey way.

Maria and I don't say anything. Katherine is totally unfazed by Beth's attitude. She smiles big and toothy and takes off for the back door. "I'll be outside smoking."

Beth shoves her hands in her back pockets. "Whatever then. I'm not going to force you guys to be here and have fun," she says in a fake-agreeable way to hide her disappointment. "I'm going to pee, drink a beer, and then we'll go."

"I'll stay if you want to stay," I concede quietly, but Beth disappears into the crowd like she doesn't hear me.

Maria must see that I'm a little upset because she tries to tickle me into smiling. While I kind of appreciate the effort, it doesn't work.

"It's not like I purposefully tried to blow it," I say. "Teddy has a girlfriend."

"Yeah, well. I don't think Teddy's your type, either."

"Exactly." I shake my head, and Maria and I both laugh a little bit.

Maria puckers her lips and blows something off my face — an eyelash, I guess. "It's a little crazy how concerned Beth can be, but remember, it's all coming from a good place." She fishes out a gold angel-wing charm necklace from the depths of her cleavage and lays it back on top of her bleach-spattered red tank top. "She just wants you to be happy."

I turn away from her and gaze off across the room. A pack of jocks have dragged an AeroBed into the middle of the room and turned it into some sort of wrestling trampoline. "Check out those guys," I say. "They just want to find an excuse to touch each other." The thought briefly crosses my mind to take a picture of them, even though they aren't my friends and the sight isn't terribly pretty. But I unzip my bag and pull out my Polaroid anyway.

"Oh my God, you are so going to be the next Diane Arbus!"

It's easy to forget that Maria is totally smart, aside from totally hot. I have no idea who Diane Arbus is, but now I'm convinced that this is going to make a hilarious picture. And messing around with my camera seems as good a distraction as a hookup. Beth had told me not to bring it, because my book bag didn't really go with my outfit. Now I'm glad I did.

I weave through the raucous crowd toward the heaving boy pile. I hold the camera up to my face and frame the shot, just as one boy wraps his legs around another's torso in what can only be described as a pretzel hold. Another guy comes up from behind and tips the guys on top of him. They are all grunting and sweating, in total testosterone heaven.

"Whoa! That's a really cool camera!"

A boy in an itchy-looking, moth-bitten green sweater and navy Dickies steps in front of my shot, totally ruining it. It's not particularly hot in the basement, but his cheeks are crisp and red. They give the impression of being freshly slapped. His wrinkly grin does little to convince me he didn't deserve it.

"Take my picture," he says, resting his chin on his fist in a cheesy Sears-portrait pose.

"What?" I take a big step back. "No."

Unfortunately, he is not deterred. In fact, his smile widens. "Well . . . then *I'll* take *your* picture." And he actually tries to grab the camera right out of my hands.

There's no way that's going to happen. So I aim and pull the trigger, just so he'll back off. Before I can say, "That'll be five dollars, jerk." He yanks the picture right out of the camera. Then he drags a squiggly line through the milky film with his finger.

"You tell me to take your picture and then you ruin it?" I'm beyond pissed off.

"Watch," he says and hands me the square. "We used to do this at art camp."

His face begins to develop, but the line he's drawn on the film doesn't. Instead, it forms the ghostly colorless outline of a bird. The shape frames his head perfectly. I look up and see the very same bird, on a yellow button the size of a quarter, pinned to the center of his plain navy-blue baseball cap. "Pretty cool, right?"

I notice now that this boy is cute. He's got a couple of light freckles that look like a dusting of cinnamon on the bridge of his nose. And even though he has plain old brown eyes, they look more sparkly than other ones I've seen.

I try to muster up some game, so I flick the button. "This is like your trademark or something?" Beth wasn't kidding. I am so bad at flirting.

"Not exactly. I have this button maker and, well, I like to make buttons." He looks down at his gray New Balances and rubs the shaggy fringe of dirty-blond hair creeping out from the band of his cap, because I guess he knows that hobby sounds sort of weird. "I made a bunch of these baby chick ones for my little cousins last Easter."

His hand dives into his back pocket and surfaces with another tiny button. He hands this one to me. It's white and says HELLO in green teacher-perfect script.

"Hello," he says.

"How many of these have you given out tonight?" I ask. I can feel myself blushing.

"Two." He grins. "I like to make friends."

"Sorry, but I can't really see you having many friends here." I don't feel like I'm going out on a limb. The other guys from Fisher Prep have congealed into tidy groups of similarities, like weight class or bad haircut. This boy doesn't fit the scene. And that definitely works in his favor.

"You're right," he tells me. Then he pulls me toward the back door.

"Wait. My friends are leaving." I try to pull free, but he's holding my hand too tight. My feet feel light and clumsy, and I bobble behind him like a balloon full of week-old helium.

"C'mon! We'll wait for them outside. Besides, I want you to meet someone."

The night is dark and dense in Teddy's manicured backyard. We waft through a cloud of smokers that congregate near the back door. One of them is Katherine. I beam my smile in her direction. She watches me through her long final drag, flicks the butt away, and goes back inside looking very unhappy. I guess she really does want to get out of here. I realize I'm squeezing this boy's hand in a hot, very sweaty vise grip. I let my hand slip free, but he catches my pinkie and links it with his.

I follow this boy down a slate path that leads toward Teddy's pool house. Automatic floodlights click on and guide our way. The sounds of bad music grow fainter with every step. I actually relax a little.

In the corner, Teddy's golden retriever lies near his doghouse, his silver chain linked to a twisted, carved topiary. When he was a puppy, Teddy would parade him hourly around our block. Now the dog is ancient, its sandy coat flecked with white hair. Nevertheless, the dog is happy to have some company. He struggles to his feet to greet us, but ultimately opts to sit and wait instead. His wagging tail sweeps aside fallen leaves from a triangle of grass.

The boy pats the dog on the head and draws me closer. He pushes back some fur. Another white HELLO button is pinned to the dog's collar.

"Wow. Making friends with the dog. We've established that this party sucks, but that's a new low."

"Tell me about it. Thank God you came along." He takes off his cap and brushes a hand through his messy, matted hair. It looks crazy choppy, like he cut it himself with those plastic scissors made for little kids. "I'm Charlie."

I smile. "What? No cute button for that, Charlie?" Now *this* feels like flirting. I think.

There's a garden bench against the pool house. We sit, and the motion lights slowly click off one by one, blacking out the path by which we came. My insides flutter.

"So are you going to tell me your name?"

Oh, right. "Ruby."

"How do you know Teddy?"

The last light over our heads clicks off and blankets us in darkness. It takes a few seconds before I can make out Charlie's shape, even though he's sitting really close to me. "I used to live a few houses down the street."

"Wait — so you don't live in Akron anymore?"

I shake my head. "I do. I just moved off this block a few years ago."

"Yeah? Why?"

I press Charlie's HELLO button into my palm until it hurts more than the answer to his question. I turn to look back at the smokers, but my eyes are still adjusting to the dark and I can't make out anything in the distance.

"Okay . . ." Charlie leans over to tie his sneaker and gives me a much needed break from his stare. "I can sense you're skeptical. You think I'm a meathead like all these other guys. Well, let me explain why I am at this lame party."

Charlie justifies his presence here. I concentrate extra hard on everything he says, trying to ice out the thoughts heating up in my brain. He goes to Fisher Prep with Teddy, but he doesn't feel like he fits in there for strikingly obvious reasons. Still, a kid has to have friends. He hates Akron, but his parents moved here this summer so his dad could start a new job.

"Rubber?" I ask.

"No," Charlie recoils at what he perceives to be an insult. "He's an art professor at Kent State. We used to live in Pittsburgh when he taught at Carnegie-Mellon. Pittsburgh was so awesome. Home of Heinz ketchup, best ketchup in the world."

Even in the dim light, I can tell his red cheeks are getting redder by the second, and I wonder if it's because I keep staring. Or if it's some kind of medical condition. Or if it's because he likes me. I should be excited. Why am I not excited?

"Ruby," he says.

I look down and see the glint of foil in his hands. A stick of gum. It might be Make-out Gum, the way he's leaning toward me really slow. But I don't want to jinx it. I'll just take the piece, chew, and see what happens.

Only, the wind picks up and my hand freezes in midair. My eyes have finally adjusted fully to the darkness. Now I can see things in the yard around us. Teddy's big crescent-shaped pool, a stack of plastic lounge chairs, a tall fence, and beyond that . . .

"Ruby, what's wrong?" Charlie asks, pulling back from me just the littlest bit.

I couldn't explain it if I wanted to, how the sight of my old house makes my body wind tighter and tighter until I'm convinced all my muscles and tendons and ligaments are seconds away from snapping. Most of the neighborhood looked unfamiliar during our ride to the party. Probably because I make it a point to completely avoid this side of town. But the orange treetop in the front yard is still the tallest one on the block. And it looks just like the tree I photographed this morning. Could that have been why I wanted to take that picture? The fall leaves are as electric as they were when I used to stare out my old bedroom window. I can see that window, too. The light is on, because someone else lives there now.

"Ruby, are you okay?"

"I'm fine," I say, even though a tear rolls down my cheek. I wipe it away as discreetly as I can and shift my body until Charlie's head blocks the view of my house behind him. "Seriously," I say. "What were we talking about?" All I can think about is my dad. All I can smell are his cigars. "Let's talk about whatever we were just talking about, okay? Please just say something."

Charlie turns his head and looks over his shoulder, then back at me, totally confused.

He probably thinks I'm crazy. He's probably right. Another couple of tears drip free, though I beg them to stay put. I try to say something, I don't even know what, but my throat closes off in a way that feels frighteningly familiar. It's not the house. It's everything else, all at once, crushing me. Everything I was hoping to escape tonight, forever. Charlie puts his gum back into his pocket. When he ducks his head, my old house appears behind him again, this time impossibly close. Like it picked itself up and moved a few feet closer. Like it's chasing me.

The dog gets up and shuffles away from us because our petting has become lazy. His movement clicks on a bright floodlight overhead, illuminating our stage. The background disappears in stark blackness, and my eyes squint to allow my pupils time to adjust.

"Ruby! We're leaving!" Beth calls from nearby.

I try to say sorry as I stand up, but I don't know if he hears me. Then I run into the blackness, gripping Beth's voice, letting the wind dry my eyes along the way. Charlie calls after me, but I don't stop. Even though running seems to do me no good at all these days.

SEVEN

It started a few months after he'd left.

Beth had a trundle bed, which was awesome for sleepovers. I never had to slum it in a sleeping bag on the floor, or spoon myself next to her and wrestle all night for covers. This bed was designated for me, the best friend, and I used it a lot — spending the night at least once every weekend and even a few times during the week, when I was particularly depressed and Mom didn't know what to do with me. Beth's home was my sanctuary then — always crowded with her two sisters and forever the right temperature of warm, the kind that made me drowsy.

That night was perfect. We'd gone bowling with her family and ate so much pizza we nearly barfed. Then Beth and I rented a bunch of our favorite movies, and Mr. Miller brought up a TV and VCR and set it up on her dresser for us. While we watched, we counted coins from the big bottle full of Miller family spare change. Beth's mom wanted to get it to the bank and said we were allowed to keep half of however much we counted and rolled. My hands smelled sharp and metallic, and no matter how much I scrubbed them, I couldn't wash away the smell. But I didn't even care. I fell asleep completely content and twenty-seven dollars richer.

It shouldn't have happened, not on a night as nice as that one.

It wasn't a typical nightmare either. I wasn't being chased by a serial killer. I didn't have to escape a fire. For the most part, everything was fine. Our house, our family. Mom, Dad, and I putting together a puzzle in the living room.

But when my dad couldn't find a particular puzzle piece from the pile, one with an edge, he suddenly got angry. He stood up and began grabbing his records from the living room shelf, while Mom kept on looking for pieces like everything was fine. I started to get worried, nervous. She handed me a puzzle piece and told me everything was going to be fine. So I forgot about Dad and started looking for an empty spot on the board.

The dream Ruby had no idea what was coming. And the dreamer Ruby, floating somewhere in the air like a ghost, unable to speak or communicate in any way, could do nothing to warn her of what was about to happen.

I woke up screaming.

Beth leapt out of bed and crouched next to me, asking what happened. Her hand touched my shoulder and she looked at her wet palm quizzically. I was completely soaked with sweat, and my legs were shaking so bad it made the sheet waver.

Beth gave me a fresh nightgown to wear. Not a crappy one, but her second-best one, with the tiny pink and blue hearts and the lace trim. I got changed in a dark corner while she pushed the trundle back underneath her mattress. She wouldn't let me sleep on it, no matter how I insisted. Instead, she scooted to the very edge of her twin bed and patted the empty space next to her until I lay back down.

EIGHT

Sweat sticks the stray hairs of my ponytail to the sides of my face as my ears search my bedroom for sounds. I'm wrinkled and warm, still dressed in last night's clothes, my left arm branded with the basket-weave impression of my scarf. I tell myself it's fine. I'm dreaming. That was absolutely not the crackle of driveway gravel.

But that doesn't satisfy me for more than a second or two. I have to check, to make sure.

I roll out of bed and race to the window in one sloppy movement. I warn myself that he won't be outside, but I still fling it open. My panting slows as I search our driveway for nonexistent tire tracks and crane my head out the window to seek imaginary red taillights.

I shiver in the cold. I am in bad shape.

By the time I reached Maria's car last night, my tears had dried. With my well-rehearsed smile, no one was the wiser that I'd been straddling hysterics mere moments before. Even though I told myself not to, I turned and looked for Charlie, but saw he'd gone. I guess that's to be expected when a strange girl cries and runs away from you when you try to kiss her.

Bypassing friendly arguments over whose turn it was, I slid into the Period Seat, cracked the window, and concentrated on the white noise of air rushing past as Maria flirted with the speed limit. Exhaustion diluted my sadness into something I could swallow. I didn't want to have any dreams that night. Only thick, black sleep.

But I wasn't that lucky.

Now, after one last look down my quiet street, I pace the perimeter of my room and let consciousness catch up with me. I'm tired of being held hostage on trips down memory lane. It's not like I'm willingly reflecting on my painful past, like Beth warned me against. I'm being completely hijacked. And I have no idea what to do to make it stop.

I just want to go back to how it was before he came. When everything was so in the past that it almost could have happened to someone else.

Part of me doesn't want to bother Beth about how I'm feeling. I mean, this is well-worn territory between us, and I doubt she could say something comforting to me that she hasn't already told me a million times before. The thing is, when friends ask you what's wrong, there's this part of them that doesn't really want to know the answer. Especially if they've seen you upset before over the same thing, again and again and again.

They'll usually give you some kind of wisdom the first time, and repeat it four or five times more, if you're lucky. I guess I'm mega-lucky, because I've heard it, on and off, for six years. But after a while, you hit a wall. If you've been given a strategy to deal with your problem, it's time to deal with the problem already.

If you don't, if you avoid changing things, it kind of becomes your own fault when they don't get better. And people will just shrug their shoulders and say patronizing things like *Are you really surprised?* or *I told you this would happen*. And then they stop feeling sorry for you.

Last night already felt kind of weird like that between me and Beth. Like because I didn't hook up with Teddy, it means I'm hell-bent on screwing myself over. Like because I didn't do exactly what she wanted, I haven't been listening to her at all.

My cordless phone chirps alive. I follow the sound and narrow in on the stubby rubber antenna poking out from under a stack of Polaroids on my nightstand. The stack is topped by a sky-blue Post-it note.

Put these somewhere other than my silverware drawer.
And plan on dinner with me tonight.

— Mom

I take the photos in one hand and the phone in the other and crash back onto my bed.

"Hello?" The smell of my own morning breath makes me wince.

"Morning, sleeeeepyhead," Beth singsongs though a sea of static — a by-product of her crappy cell phone and our even crappier cordless.

"Hey!" I perk up at the sound of her voice. "I was just thinking about you."

"Creepy," she says and laughs.

I am so glad to hear that laugh. It means that the tension of last night is forgotten and things between us are okay. "Have you eaten?" I wedge the receiver between the side of my head and my shoulder and flip through the photos. Mom, Beth, Katherine, Maria. I tentatively flip to the next one. Jim looks ghostly, framed in our front doorway, with sallow skin against the night sky, an expressionless face, mouth slightly agape. There's a blur over the collar of his flannel coat. I tilt the photo underneath a ray of sunlight. The mark is a slender almond-shaped fingerprint. My mother's. I don't want to think about her lingering over his face. So I shuffle him quickly to the bottom.

"Nope. Have you?"

"No. And I'm totally starving. Let's go to Dodie's. My treat." My stomach growls at the thought of a mountain of extra-crispy home fries drizzled with ketchup.

"Rain check on that. Maria's picking us up to go Halloween-costume shopping in a half hour. I'll be over in about five minutes. With breakfast." She rings her bike bell three times for me.

"Awesome." My throat tightens, pleading for me to stop there, but I force myself to keep talking. After all, Beth is my best friend. Even if it frustrated her, she'd want to know if I wasn't okay. "Ride like the wind, all right? Because I'd like to talk to you before everyone gets here."

"Why? Did something happen?" Her words drip out cautiously.

"Nah. Just wanted your opinion on this thing," I say casually, as if debating over two flavors of ice cream. "Listen, I'm gonna jump in the shower, so go ahead and let yourself in."

"I'm on my way." Wind whips against her phone as she pedals faster.

I hang up and reach around to my back pocket. Charlie's portrait is bent and crinkled from a night's worth of sleep in my jeans. The tragedy of us makes him even cuter, if that's possible. I thread his HELLO button through the white frame border, put him at the very top, and slide the whole stack underneath my pillow.

The leg hair I avoided yesterday prickles up when I strip. Our bathroom is always chilly, because my mom mandates the window be open a crack to keep mildew from spotting the ceiling. I crank the hot water and pull the razor though the thick cream in long, confident ankle-to-thigh avenues. I brush my teeth, comb all the knots out of my long dark hair, pair some clean clothes Mom left folded in the laundry basket with my forever dirty Levi's, and bound downstairs. I don't know why, but just thinking about talking to Beth is making me feel better than I have in days.

I greet her before I walk into the kitchen, but she's not waiting for me like she should be. The clock over the sink reads 10:45 A.M. — it's been about twenty minutes since we hung up the phone and Maria would be arriving in another ten. Our tiny kitchen feels cavernous.

I fetch the cordless and dial Beth's cell, planning to tease her with some defective Akron-made-bike-tire joke in case she got a flat on her way over. A muffled rendition of the "Peanuts" theme song trickles in from the living room. Beth's ring tone. I follow it past the couch and over to the window, where I peek out the blinds.

Beth's rusty ten-speed is up on its kickstand next to our holly bush. She's sitting hunched over on my front stoop with her head down, curls dribbling over her striped sweater and into her face. Between her curtain of hair and the angle I'm at, I can't tell if she's sleeping or crying or fraying the thin spots on her jeans with her fingernails. The twinkling lights from her cell phone glow out of her back pocket until my unanswered call goes to voice mail. I do not leave a message.

I pull the door open quietly so I won't scare her. A triangular flock of birds headed south screeches above us and gives me away.

She leaps up and spins around, both of her hands diving deep into her back pockets. "Geez, Ruby!" she gasps, as if I were spying on her or something.

"Are you okay?" I say, stepping outside. The sun is bright, but the air is still crisp and cold. "I just called you but you didn't answer."

Beth rocks back and forth on her heels and tips her head back in a casual stretch. "You did? I'm sorry. I guess I zoned out. Anyhow, I rang your doorbell a few times, but you were still in the shower."

I bend over the metal railing and reach up around the corner of the awning, pawing the sandpapery shingles. "Why didn't you use the spare key?" We've always hidden a spare to our house. Beth uses it often. The jagged edge of metal ribs my fingertip and I produce a gold key in the palm of my hand.

Beth takes the key and examines it in the light like the Giant Eagle cashiers do to twenty-dollar bills. "Huh. Must have missed it. Your arms are way longer than mine, remember." She tucks the key back in its hiding place and sashays past me into the house toting a white paper bag. The buttery deliciousness of fresh Leetch's raspberry jelly donuts wafts behind her. I follow her inside.

Beth drops the bag on the kitchen table. The grease bleeds translucent polka dots. I sink into a seat and hear the *whoosh whoosh whoosh* of her shaking up a quart of orange juice behind me. She pours us each a glass.

"Thanks, Mom," I joke, and try to toss it back with one swallow. A blob of pulp rolls down my thermal. Beth hands me a wet paper towel and sits quietly as I dab the spots.

When I look up from my shirt, Beth's staring off blankly out the kitchen window. I know I made my topic of conversation sound trivial over the phone, and I guess her lack of urgency is my own fault. I start talking, but not about what's on my mind, exactly. I suddenly feel like I have to warm up to that conversation.

"Is there anything special you want for your birthday? I'm stumped on what to get you." I dig inside the bag for a donut. It feels heavy and warm in my hand.

Beth grabs one and chomps into it, spraying a puff of powdered sugar into the air. Then she reclines against the counter. "I don't know. How about you take a special picture for me or something homemade like that," she says through bites. A little jelly trickles out the corner of her mouth and she catches it with her tongue.

She smiles when she realizes I've been watching her. But it's not her normal toothy variety. This one is long and thin and taut. I drop my chin to my chest. When Beth's paying attention, she can read me like a book. And it's finally hit her that something's wrong.

"You heard from him again," she whispers.

I shake my head. "No. You're right. He's probably long gone, off to who knows where by now." It's crazy. I wonder if he even knows how much he's messed up my life after his stupid five-minute visit. Probably not.

Beth stares down at the remainder of her donut and then takes her last bites with a pensive look. "Okay. Is this about last night? Because I'm really sorry if I pushed you too hard with

Teddy. You know I was just trying to take your mind off things. I had good intentions." She wrings her hands.

I meet her face and force a smile. "No, I don't care about that. It was a good plan. Just the wrong boy."

"What about that other guy? The one Katherine saw you talking to outside."

"Yeah," I say wistfully. "I screwed that up." My body temperature ignites. Just say it. "That's kind of what I wanted to talk to you about. Because I think maybe there's something to what you said in the gym."

Beth shakes her head slowly. "What do you mean? What did I say?"

I take a deep breath. And then a deeper one. "That I have a phobia about hooking up. But I think it's bigger than that." My mouth feels sticky. Each syllable requires incredible effort. "I think I've still got major problems."

The wrinkles in Beth's forehead smooth out and her head drops slightly to the left. "Ruby, I didn't really mean what I said . . ."

"I know. I know you were only kidding. But I think there might be some truth in it, unfortunately." Before I can stop myself, I pour out the story of last night. Of seeing my old house again and completely freaking out. How I'm the only one of our friends who's never hooked up before. How I'm so afraid I'm going to end up alone like my mother. How I don't even know what it was that sent my dad away, and now I'll never know what it was that brought him back. How I've been inundated with flashbacks, forgotten memories of him leaving that are billowing up inside my brain, hurting me all over again.

Her bottom lip starts to quiver.

"Beth — " I say, with a desperate laugh to keep her from crying. I absolutely hate it when Beth cries.

She leans over the table and her tears pitter-patter onto the empty paper bag. When she looks up at me, her face is flush and wet. "I feel so guilty." Her chest heaves up and down with jagged breaths.

"Why would you feel guilty?"

Her eyes are red and frightened, like a rabbit. "Because I'm a bad friend."

"That's crazy," I say, sliding my chair next to hers. "Without you, I wouldn't have gotten through all this in the first place. Lord knows my mom had no idea what to do with me, and those hokey school counselors only wanted me to recount every stupid little detail about all the terrible stuff I was feeling. Those were the worst hours of my life. But you always found a way to distract me."

She tips her head back and smiles, though the tears keep falling in fat splashes. "Remember how we made that voodoo doll out of your dad's old sock and stuck him with pins from my dad's toolbox?" She laughs, and a little bubble of snot sprouts at the edge of her nostril. "That's some nontraditional therapy right there."

"Or how we'd make potions out of hair spray and cough syrup and Tilex to poison him with if he ever came back?" Seriously. We'd dump the entire contents of her medicine cabinet into a jelly jar and leave it to bake in a sunny patch on the side of her garage for months.

"Or that fake report card I made when you did that oral report on the Underground Railroad in Mrs. Loughlin's class?"

I smile. The faded piece of blue construction paper with the red letter A that Beth slipped into my backpack. I hadn't spoken in class for about a year and it was becoming a real problem. I had weekly appointments with the guidance counselor, which I hated more than anything. There was even some talk of putting me on medication. Beth told me that the sooner I could show everyone I was better, the less I'd have to deal with the people who wanted me to rehash my sad feelings all the time. She was so proud of me for standing up in front of the whole class and speaking as loud and steady as I could. I remember seeing Mrs. Loughlin's jaw drop in surprise, as well as a bunch of the other kids who thought I was mute or something. Beth gave me two big thumbs up from behind her workbook. It was like she was the only one there.

Beth takes a deep breath and wriggles out of her striped sweater. "I know things have been crazy the last forty-eight hours, and it's brought up a lot of old crap from the past that we'd both like to forget, but you have to trust me, Ruby. Your dad's gone now, and things are going to go back to normal. You've just got to push all this out of your head."

"Do you really think?"

She nods. "It's like people who have had family members die . . . they always get sad around the holidays. It doesn't mean they haven't come to terms with them being gone. This is just a hiccup, like that. Nothing more." Her eyes jump all over my face. "Promise that you believe me."

"Okay," I say. I want to believe her.

She shakes her head. "No. You need to promise."

I pull away from her and place my hand over my heart, like I'm saying the Pledge of Allegiance. "I promise." Maybe it isn't quite true, but it certainly feels good to hear someone tell you that you're not a mess. At least with Beth on my side, I know I can get through this. After all, I did it once before.

Maria's horn beeps from outside. I clear the table, put our juice glasses into the sink, and grab my old ski vest, while Beth dries her face on her sleeve. On our way to the front door, she sinks me to the carpet with a huge hug.

Somehow I feel lighter.

NINE

You'd never mistake Goodwill for a department store, because of the smell. It's like opening a trunk of sweaters during August. Or taking a walk though the historic home of Rutherford B. Hayes, where the windows never open and old reading glasses are fastened permanently to a nightstand. It's the scent of quiet. Everything's stale and muted. I think it's the best smell in the world.

Beth spends the entire drive over prepping us on our mission, which she's broken down into bullet points in her party-planning notebook. Since we're her closest friends, she wants to make sure we have cool costumes, and if we need her help or advice, we should feel free to ask. We are also informed that anyone not wearing a costume will be forbidden entry. Unlike years past, cheap plastic masks from the drugstore will not be acceptable, nor will the old "I'm dressing up as myself" excuse. There has to be some level of *trying* involved, the discretion of which is up to her. Beth reasons that if people don't take their costumes seriously, then they won't be taking her birthday seriously either and don't deserve to be there. After all, turning sixteen is a pretty big deal and she isn't going to let anything or anyone ruin it for her. Which makes sense, I guess.

Once we get to Goodwill, an overstuffed rack of T-shirts spreads out before me like a horizontal rainbow. I thrust my hip inside the tightly packed orange area to create a little shuffle room and flip through the wares, looking for nothing in particular but hoping the official color of Halloween will inspire my hunt for a costume. I pass by a couple of so-sos and some no-nos before I double-take at a retro Cleveland Browns shirt the color of Sunkist mixed with melted ice cubes. The insignia flakes off around the upper-left corner, there's a grass stain across the back, and the armpits are nearly see-through. It's impossibly soft. I check the collar — *Youth Large.* $2.99 on a blue paper tag means it's half-off on Saturday. All these reasons lumped together deem it total thrift-store gold.

I rise on my toes and watch the top of Beth's head drift down a fluorescent-lit aisle. I follow the runner of brown industrial carpet into the skirt section, waving my find over my head in victory.

"Umm, I think I've found the best shirt ever!"

A few heads turn toward me, annoyed. The novelty of retro is lost on people who ignore the smell and make this place a department store out of necessity. I permanently lower my voice.

Beth inspects the shirt with a raised eyebrow while I get lost in the multitude of fabrics thrown over her shoulder. There's a polyester skirt, a corduroy jacket, an old satiny slip, some wool leggings, and a shimmery scarf. I wish I felt safe in fabrics other than cotton.

"Hmm . . . okay. Yeah. This can work," she says, nodding with approval. "We can get you some white sweatpants and paint black stripes under your eyes. I have no idea where you'll find a football helmet. Or shoulder pads. We could use some rolled-up towels for that, I guess. But you definitely need a helmet if you want to have the whole look. Without the helmet, it isn't going to work. So maybe you should think about a backup, just in case."

"Not for a costume," I say, holding the shirt up against my chest. "For the other three hundred and sixty-four days of the year."

Beth groans and walks toward the ladies' dressing room we've commandeered. "Ruby, I really need you to focus, all right?" she whines. "My party is exactly one week away!"

"Okay. Sorry," I say. "I'll focus." If only I had some ideas to focus on. But coming to Goodwill makes me feel like I've got attention deficit disorder. Colors grab and lose my attention; quirky fonts on the tags, missing buttons, strange sizes. I get lost in the idea of who wore these clothes in a former life. Like the Cleveland Browns shirt. This boy loved football and wrestled out on the lawn with his dad as he fought for the last few yards of a driveway touchdown. I can seriously see them in my mind, like a picture.

Maria's squeal drifts from an aisle near the plate-glass windows. As I take off in her direction, an arm reaches out and grabs my elbow, pulling me to a stop.

"Slow down there!" a crackly old voice whines.

"Oh, excuse me," I say, and whirl around to find Katherine swathed in a tent-sized Hawaiian-print muumuu, arched over like the letter n. Her spine straightens out and she takes off past me, cackling like a wicked witch and calling me a word that no proper old lady would ever use.

Maria's posing in front of a mirrored column. She's got a terry-cloth band around her head and a white pleated skirt on a hanger threaded in her belt loop, so it drapes against her frame like a paper doll's clothes. It is exactly the same length as the pleated skirt she already has on. She swings a vintage wooden tennis racket over her shoulder. "All this, plus my favorite pink polo. Ta-da!"

"I don't get it," Katherine says sarcastically, falling against the mirror and blocking Maria's view of herself. "If you want to dress up like something different for Halloween, you should be a nun. A nun with a chastity belt."

"I'd still get more attention than you in your old-lady costume," Maria sasses.

Katherine pulls the muumuu over her head and hurls it at a nearby rack. "This isn't my costume."

"Well, Beth's not going to let you in without one. Remember?"

Katherine rolls her eyes. "Isn't dressing up for Halloween a little junior high? I mean, the whole cold-spaghetti-in-a-bowl thing loses its fear factor when you stop being afraid of the dark."

I hang the muumuu back up with a spare hanger. I should tell Katherine that Beth doesn't take many things more seriously than she does her Halloween/birthday party. She transforms her basement into a highly stylized haunted house, not some hokey G-rated playhouse with goody bags and homemade chocolate lollipops. She knows a butcher who sells her actual cow tongues that she uses for a centerpiece. The guest list is limited to the cool kids in Beth's art electives and the cutest guys in Maria's phone-book. (I could invite whomever, but everyone's usually been accounted for.) And this year, after the success of Katherine's sto-len champagne at my party, Beth has convinced her sister Suzy to buy us some raspberry vodka and hide it in the bottom of her dirty-laundry bag, which Beth and her oblivious mom will pick up tonight from Suzy's Cleveland State dorm. But I don't say anything. Let Katherine think we're junior high. She can go ahead and not come. We'd all have a better time without her.

Beth emerges from the dressing room and flags us over. She's wearing a plain black slip.

"Naughty housewife?" Maria asks. "I love it!"

Beth studies herself in the mirror with a big smile, seeing something different than we do in her reflection. "I've got big plans for this little black slip." Beth's costumes are always over-the-top, with weeks of effort and custom-made touches behind each one. She's a little behind this year, but I have no doubt she'll turn it into something amazing. Her attention shifts to the rest of us. "Maria, I absolutely love it! The vintage racket is an awesome touch. Great job." She gives Maria a big hug and they both bounce up and down. "Now, how about you two?"

"I've got my costume all planned at home," Katherine says. "Trust me, you'll love it!" She pretends to be really interested in a men's bathing suit so she doesn't have to make eye contact.

"Ruby, you better pick your costume quick, because I've gotta be home soon. Davey's picking me up at six to go to see his brother's band play. He's got us on the list, so we don't need ID." Maria checks her phone and pounds out an urgent-looking text message.

Beth rolls her eyes. She obviously thinks Maria's wasting her time.

I stammer and look around at the big store. It's more like a warehouse, really. A warehouse of possibilities. It's daunting.

"All right, Miss Indecisive." Beth laughs and playfully bumps my hip. "I've got a plan. Everyone pick out a costume for Ruby. There'll be a two-minute time limit. Then bring your choice back into the dressing room and she'll have to pick one of them as the winner." She turns to me. "Okay?"

"But what if I don't like any of them?" I ask.

Beth smiles. "Shut up! You totally will." She cocks her hand into the shape of a gun. "On your mark. Get set."

"Wait!" My eyes travel from her bare feet up skinny legs to the hem of the slip. "Aren't you going to change first?"

Beth fires into the air. "Go!"

Everyone takes off in a fever, including Katherine. I doubt she cares what costume I wear; she's just competitive. I stand at the open door of our dressing room and check my wristwatch. I spin a rack of silk scarves like a pinwheel.

"Ninety seconds left!" I call out.

"What size pants are you?" Katherine shouts.

"I don't know. Medium? Or a six?"

"Are you opposed to trying something a little sexier than you're used to?" Maria calls out.

"No participant feedback allowed!" Beth shouts.

One by one, the girls dash past me and hang up their selections inside the dressing room. I cover my face with my hands so I can't see who's bringing what, though I'm sure I'll be able to figure it out anyway. When the time is up, I am pushed inside and the white slatted door bangs closed behind me.

"Now strip!" Maria shouts.

Beth's clothes are already in a heap on the floor, so I push them into the corner. I peel off my ski vest, thermal T-shirt, and jeans and place them on top of her pile.

They all titter outside — I peer down and see Katherine's Pumas, Maria's checkerboard Vans, and Beth's bare feet, all in a row, waiting for my decision.

Hanging on a hook to my right is a pair of light blue terry-cloth shorts with a rainbow-colored heart on each butt cheek. Wait, no. It's one of those one-piece jumpsuits from the seventies. I try it on for fun because it would be cool to dress like Maria for a night, and have the confidence to work the room. But I don't look sexy and curvy like her. I am thin and pointy and don't have nearly enough boobs to keep the top afloat.

"I couldn't find roller skates to go with my selection, but it's supposed to have roller skates!" Maria calls out.

"Okay!" I quickly peel it off and hang it back on the hook. Now I'm worried.

Then I spot a little short-sleeve button-up shirt hanging on the back of the door. It's white, with a tiny green pattern made by the repeating face of the Girl Scout logo. The one on that yummy shortbread cookie.

I button up the shirt okay, but it buckles when I stand up straight, leaving three little gaps where my bra is visible. I could wear a shirt underneath, I guess. The cap sleeves cut into my arm meat like rubber bands, but I figure a few snips along the inside seams will loosen them up. A stiff green skirt accompanies the look, and although I pretty much only wear jeans, I'd consider going the extra mile for this costume. It's a little short, grazing the middle of my thigh, but the waistband fits comfortably. I slip the blank green sash over my head and realize I'll have to make my own badges and I'm nowhere near as artistic or craft-savvy as Beth is, but maybe that could be fun. Or something we could do together.

Overall, the costume needs some work. I'll need to get knee socks and maybe a beret. And I sort of look like I suffer from a hormone growth disorder. Still, I've always wanted to be a Girl Scout. There's something so wholesome, so honest about them. It could be a statement, the reclamation of my lost youth. Whatever. It's a hands-down winner.

I step out of the dressing room beaming.

Katherine steps forward and pushes me hard on the shoulder. "Looks like I know you best!" She beams a shit-eating grin.

"What?" I say.

Beth's face puckers. "How could you not like my punk rock getup? I even made sure there was a T-shirt, so you'd feel comfortable!"

I look back into the dressing room. Beth's selection—a pair of ripped-up acid-washed jeans and an old Misfits shirt—hangs untouched on a hook near the mirror.

"I played up the sentimental angle. You know, her whole shattered childhood mentality," Katherine brags to the group, like I'm not even there. "Worked like a charm."

I duck back into the dressing room and slam the door behind me.

"Oh, Ruby, relax," Katherine says. "It's just a costume."

"A really cute costume," Maria offers.

I'm on fire with anger, manipulated and tricked by my own stupid past. I kick the pile of clothes on the floor and it flies apart.

My jeans land with Beth's and I kick them again, for good measure. That's when I see it. Half of an envelope sliding out of Beth's back pocket.

I pinch the corner between two fingers and slide it out the rest of the way, careful, like it's hot or something. The blue ink vibrates blurry letters until I lean against the wall to settle my trembling arms.

Although the envelope is addressed to *Rubes*, it's already been opened by someone else. By her.

TEN

Dear Rubes,

I hope your mom told you this already, but I'm real sorry about ruining your birthday party. One more thing to add to the list of stupid things I've done, I guess.

I know your head is probably swimming just like mine. Lots of questions and crazy thoughts. There's so much we never had the chance to talk about and a lot that's hard to understand.

I've decided to take a week and stay in Akron before I get reassigned. Maybe you'll come see me before I check out next Saturday night. But if I don't hear from you, I'll figure you officially want nothing to do with me and I won't contact you again.

I'm staying at the Holiday Inn, near the highway. Room 435.

Dad

ELEVEN

Just as my eyes roll along the inky script of my dad's signature, three rapid-fire knocks drum on the dressing room door.

"Hey!" Beth calls out all friendly and sweet. "Can I come in and change?"

I haven't seen his handwriting in forever. Something about the small, scratchy, impatient penmanship looks similar to my own, but there's no time to study the similarities. I tear my eyes away, and the floor undulates beneath my feet.

My dad did not go back to Oregon. He's here, in Akron. He's waiting for me. I wasn't dreaming after all. Those were his tires I heard crunching the driveway gravel this morning. He must have left the letter for me on the front stoop. And that's where Beth found it this morning, and that's why she acted all weird and upset. It all makes perfect sense.

Except for the part where Beth doesn't show me the letter and hides it from me instead. That makes absolutely no sense to me at all.

The metal hook wiggles inside its eyehole as Beth tugs on the handle from the other side. Her shadowy outline is visible through the white slatted door. She cups her hands and tries to peek through. "C'mon, Ruby," she says insistently. "I've seen you in your underwear a million times."

The last thing I want is to be caught red-handed. The paper sticks to my clammy hands like it doesn't want me to let go. I fold it up and tuck it quietly back inside the envelope. Beth's stuff lies in a tangle at my feet. I crouch down, shove the envelope deep into the back pocket of her jeans, and kick everything aside. Beth's bag overturns in the process and her party-planning notebook and pen slide out. I quickly scribble his room number on the inside of my wrist in the smallest writing possible. Then I unhook the latch, open the dressing room door, and stuff my finger into my mouth.

Beth's brow furrows as her hazel eyes take me in. She steps forward and locks the door quickly behind her. "Katherine really upset you, huh?" Her hand wafts around the general area of my face. "Ruby, I know it wasn't funny, but she really was just joking with you."

I unbutton the Girl Scout shirt and twist to face the mirror. Blotches of angry redness creep up my neck to my ears. I unwind the hair band from the base of my ponytail and let my thick dark hair cloak me. It feels cool and safe behind the curtain. "No. I'm fine. It's just a little stuffy in here or something." My voice sounds strange and disembodied.

We change in silence, back-to-back, while blood vessels continue to pop open all over my body. I concentrate on taking deep breaths, but infuriating questions keep trying to choke me. Why is he so hell-bent on seeing me now? Couldn't he tell from the way things went down on my birthday that I don't want anything to do with him? And why hasn't Beth said anything to me yet? Because every minute she doesn't mention it, she's basically lying to me.

Beth's silk slip rustles as it slides over her head. A few sparks of static electricity crackle through her auburn waves. "Listen, I didn't mean to snap at you about the whole costume thing." She steps into her beyond-skinny pencil-leg jeans and jumps a few times as she pulls them up to her waist. "As stupid as it sounds, I didn't want Katherine to win. I wanted to be the one who knew you best."

I don't say anything. I just wait and wait and wait for her to tell me already. I can hear her breathing. Each inhale sounds deep, like the kind you take at the start of a sentence. But she doesn't say anything. She just keeps breathing and I keep waiting. "Beth. I — " I force myself to look at her straight on, but my eyes quickly return to the dirty carpet. When? When is she going to say something?

"Don't even say it, because I know I'm acting crazy. You'll be a super cute Girl Scout. I'd buy, like, a million boxes of cookies from you."

I am so confused I can't think straight. I step into my dirty gray New Balances and tie them up. Beth, already dressed, bends down to give each of my shoes a precautionary double knot. My eyes ride the curve of her spine to the back pockets of her jeans. I can't see the letter, or even make out its general shape through the denim.

Beth smiles at me, hopeful. "So we're cool?"

I nod. It's all I can manage at the moment.

Beth unlatches the door and holds it open for me. As soon as I step into the store, Katherine bolts out from behind a shelf of tattered and yellowed paperback novels. She positions herself directly in front of me and pulls the tip of her long ponytail out of her mouth. The blond hair is dark and wet with saliva.

"Ruby, hey," Katherine says. "Listen, I want to apologize."

I walk straight past her and make my way to the cashier with my costume wadded up in one hand and a few dollar bills in the other. My dad probably wants to apologize too. Use my forgiveness to ease his own guilt or something like what Beth had said that night at the park. Unfortunately, I'm not feeling particularly merciful. I'm even tired of feeling sorry for myself.

Katherine sulks the whole ride home in the Period Seat. I sit next to her and ignore her funk, in favor of watching the passing cars and analyzing and breaking down the entire situation to help me understand what's going on. I decide that Beth hasn't said anything because the other girls are here. She's waiting to tell me once we're alone. That would make sense. She's probably sitting in the front seat, trying to figure out exactly how she should break the news.

When Maria drives up Magnolia Hill, I can see the big sign of the Holiday Inn in the distance. It has to be about five miles away from my house, tops. I imagine Jim waiting there, wondering if I got his letter. Waiting to see if I'll show up. Beth fiddles with the radio in the passenger seat. She doesn't see the hotel. She's not even looking.

Maria drops me and Beth off at my house. We walk up the stone path together, our feet moving at the same gait, but the space between us is as wide as my street. I'm holding my breath in anticipation. It's going to happen now. It's got to happen right now.

"I wish I wasn't going to Suzy's tonight," she laments. "If it weren't for the liquor, I'd tell my mom to go without me. I'm already paranoid enough about getting caught, but I think it'll be worth it, don't you? I mean, parties at our age are a little babyish if you don't have any alcohol." Beth's green ten-speed is still up on its kickstand near the front door, and the afternoon breeze has netted a few fallen leaves in the spokes. She drops her plastic bag of clothes in the wire bike basket and stoops over to pick the leaves out.

I kneel down next to Beth and run my hands lightly over the tips of the grass. The cold seeps through my jeans and ices my knees. Maybe in her own weird way, Beth is trying to protect me. She's always telling me to forget things, to let them go and move on. And the thing is, if I had been the one to find the letter, I would have shown it to Beth first thing and asked her what she thought of it, what I should do. Maybe Beth is trying to save me from some emotional stress. If I hadn't freaked out in the kitchen this morning, she might have shown me Jim's letter. She still might. She might just be waiting for the perfect time.

Why isn't this the perfect time?

Beth stands up and extends her hand. She grips mine, firm and sure, and pulls me to my feet. "I'll have my cell on me the whole night. Call if you need anything. Seriously, anything at all." She straddles her bike. "And remember — you have nothing to worry about."

"Okay." I stuff my hands into the pockets of my ski vest.

She takes off, pedaling down the walkway and jumping the curb into the street. I watch her weave around potholes and parked cars until she gets to the end of the block. There, she rings her bell and waves a last good-bye over her shoulder before disappearing around the corner.

I stand on my front lawn, completely stunned, for I don't know how long. Beth's taken one day away from my potential reunion. Seven days are left for her to come clean about the letter, seven days for me to figure out how to act normal and pretend like everything's okay until she does.

TWELVE

Mom is definitely up to something. She keeps coming upstairs to stick her head in my room and make a weird face and utter a completely non-scary Halloween sound. Imagine a kindergarten teacher channeling the ghost of a kitten. Then she cracks herself up and bounds back down the steps.

It's too corny not to laugh. But somehow I manage to keep it together. Whenever my mom acts all silly, I get automatically serious. It's like a reflex. And tonight, of all nights, I'm just not in the mood to joke around. I don't know why she'd be either, unless it's to convince me that things around here are officially Back to Normal. Or maybe she's seen Jim again herself, or she knows about the letter he left for me and hopes I'll bring it up. Sorry, but that's not going to happen.

My room vibrates in sync with her footsteps. She's coming to haunt my bedroom again. I grab my camera and snap her picture as she cranes her head around the door, so I can show her how dumb she's acting. For some reason the Polaroid develops all weird and smoky, which only eggs her on.

"You can't photograph a ghost!" she cries, dancing around me in a circle.

That's what they say about vampires. Not ghosts. But I am more concerned about my camera possibly being messed up than about correcting her mistake. So I sit down at my desk, inspect the rollers, and ignore her.

We don't eat together all that often and especially not on the weekends, when she picks up extra shifts at the hospital. Usually I'm out with Beth and the girls by the time she gets home from work. Sometimes I offer to stay home and hang out with her, if there's nothing else really going on, but she says she likes the quiet time. She watches whatever old movies are on television, tries a new flavor of fancy tea that she buys from the hospital gift shop, or gives her hair a hot oil treatment.

When we do have dinner together, she likes to make it a big production. She'll use a meticulously snipped recipe from a magazine, featuring some crazy ingredient that we have to ask someone at the grocery store courtesy desk to help us find. The table gets set with the fancy porcelain plates that we keep stacked in the back of the linen closet. She'll pull her brown hair up in little twists and folds and sit across from me in a shirt that's too pretty for the hospital. Occasionally, she'll even light a candle. I always blow it out before I sit down. I don't mean to be a jerk, but there's something creepy about having a dinner date with your mom.

It's pretty obvious why she does it. She doesn't have much of a life. Which sucks. Dating would be good for her, and me too, I think. Not that I want her to act like Maria or anything. I see a montage of bed-and-breakfasts, wine tastings, watching the trees change colors, and other grown-up date activities. With one nice guy she could settle down with.

It wouldn't be hard for her to meet someone. She's young and pretty, in an honest, wholesome, Ohio-ish divorced mom way. Shiny hair and apple cheeks and toned limbs. Which makes it all the more sad that she shuts herself down every time a man's eyes linger over her a few seconds longer than she thinks they should.

One time a man hit on her while we were waiting for his parking spot at the post office. It was completely embarrassing, and I would have crawled into the glove compartment, had it been possible. He cooed that he'd seen her around town and had always wanted to introduce himself. You could tell by the way he leaned his arm up on the top of our car roof that he liked her.

He wasn't sleazy. He was a professional, wearing a tie and flat-front navy-blue pants that rippled in the spring breeze. He seemed nice enough, and handsome too. Definitely taller than Jim. And stronger. His teeth were white and straight and friendly, not yellowed from cheap cigars.

Mom wasn't having it. As soon as he started talking, her top lip curled up, like she'd just popped a sour candy into her mouth. "Not in front of my daughter," she hissed, before rolling up her window and peeling out. We bought our stamps at the 7-Eleven down the road that day, and rode home in complete silence.

We're like old war buddies. We have history and love and camaraderie, but neither of us wants to relive the battles we've been through or compare how the pink, tough skin of our scars hasn't softened over time. We're content to let our past hang heavy between us without comment, and breathe shallowly around it. Neither of us wants to trigger a painful flashback.

Mom finally calls me for dinner. Before I go downstairs, I reset the camera and hold it up to my face. The flash blinds and stings, but the film develops okay. It captures my eyes a second before I squint. My pupils look bigger than usual, like they are desperate to drink in the light. Like I am empty.

The kitchen microwave dings and announces my arrival.

"Hope you don't mind leftovers," Mom says as she pulls two steaming plates of my birthday ziti out of the microwave. She turns first to the kitchen table and, forgetting for a second that she covered it in old newspaper for whatever reason, sets them down on a tiny spread of countertop instead.

I don't mind leftovers at all. Ziti is always better after a day of sitting in the fridge. But tonight's dinner is a lot more casual than I was expecting. I drop into a seat and glance down at a spread of grocery store coupons, feeling a bit suspicious. "What's all this for?"

Mom whips around from the kitchen sink wielding a huge knife and an evil grin. She looks like a patient escaped from a mental ward in her green nursing scrubs and with all the flyaway pieces poking out of her ponytail. She stalks over to where I'm sitting, hoists a heavy brown paper bag onto the table, and stabs at it with serial-killer intensity.

I push my chair back until I'm butted up against the cabinets.

Mom pauses to admire her reflection in the blade. "Did I scare you?"

I roll my eyes and ignore the beads of sweat bubbling up on the back of my neck.

She cackles and raises the knife high over her head again. This time, she slices the bag into four wide petals and peels them back to reveal two dirty pumpkins. Then she waits for my big reaction, with raised, expectant, perfectly plucked eyebrows.

"Yay." It comes out even more unenthusiastic than I mean it to. But carving pumpkins seems like a weird, sentimental thing for us to be doing together.

"What? What's wrong with pumpkin carving? Halloween is only a week away!" Her voice sheds its playfulness in favor of annoyance.

She won't take her eyes off me, so I lean over, pull open the junk drawer, and paw through until I find a Magic Marker. "Nothing's wrong with pumpkin carving."

Her face eases back into a smile when she sees I'll play along. "I think we missed out on lots of trick-or-treaters the last few years because the house wasn't properly decorated." She pats her amazingly flat stomach. "And I can't handle another year of having to eat all those leftover Kit Kats from Giant Eagle."

I don't buy that as her real reason, exactly. But I don't think she knows anything about the letter, either. This activity seems more about me and her than us and him.

Mom lays out a selection of knives, finds a baking sheet for the seeds, and pulls over the trash can. "I got inspired today when I saw this idea on television in a patient's room," she says, easing into the seat across from me and reaching out for the smaller of the two pumpkins. She lays it on its side and lets the gnarled green stem jut outward. "You make the stem into a nose and carve a face around it. Isn't this one just perfect for that?"

"It might be hard to light a candle in there, though." I reach out and give her pumpkin a little tap. It spins across the table.

"Hmm." She picks up her pumpkin and cradles it in her hands. A few flecks of dirt fall onto her lap. The corners of her mouth sink.

"You can still do it that way, Mom. I didn't mean to say — "

"No, I think you have a point." She takes out her ponytail holder and puts her hair back up, smoothing it neater than before.

I shouldn't ruin her fun. She has so little of it. I try to shake off my bad mood and have a good time for her sake. "Okay. Well, if you do a grin, I'll do a frown. Then we can sit them on opposite sides of our stairs."

She nods at me, reaches for one of the smaller knives, and starts sawing in a circle.

We scrape out the guts and free the seeds from the slimy tentacles. Mom manages to stay remarkably clean, while the front of my white tee gets splattered in wet orange pulp. Neither of us is really talking. Every time I look at her, she's already staring at me, wearing a sort of sad-looking smile, like the kind people wear at funerals when someone's telling them a nice story about the person who died.

"What costume are you wearing to Beth's party?" Mom asks as she leans over to turn on the stove for her kettle.

I've drawn a pretty awesome-looking frown on my pumpkin. It stretches all the way across the front, and it's made up of long, skinny rectangles, like the grate of a scary basement furnace. I just need the right knife to start carving. Something small and delicate. "I found an old Girl Scout uniform at the thrift store today."

Mom gasps and closes her eyes for a few seconds, like she's dreaming. "You always wanted to be a Girl Scout! Will you try it on for me?"

"Maybe later." I push the knife in all the way, and apply slow and steady pressure down on the handle, trying my best to slice in a straight line.

"You were too shy, back then, for such a big group." She takes the saltshaker and gives the seeds a good coating before popping them in the oven.

Too shy is how my mom likes to describe what happened to me after Jim left. Which I find equal parts irritating and hilarious. I mean, I'm all about not dealing with reality, but come on. "It wasn't that I was shy, Mom." I raise my eyes the littlest bit from my pumpkin and watch her face for a reaction. "You know that. I went crazy."

She hums to herself as she draws a big smiley face, like she didn't even hear me. "You could join the Girl Scouts now, if you wanted to."

"Umm. I don't think so." My hands are still slimy and I'm having some trouble holding on to my pumpkin, so I cradle it in between my legs, using them as a vise.

"Oh, but you can! They have it for older girls. It's like the Eagle Scouts. Except not that, exactly. I don't know what they call it for the girls. Maybe the Eaglettes?"

"Mom, I don't want to be a teenage Girl Scout. It's just a Halloween costume."

She rests her marker on the table and looks at me, like I've done something wrong. "You can do anything you want to do, Ruby. That's all I'm trying to say."

I know she means well by orchestrating this mother-daughter time, and pumpkin carving is kind of a fun thing to do after all, I guess. I don't mean to be edgy or impatient with her. It's just that I find her motivational speeches pretty meaningless. It's obvious that Jim's presence is as tangible as if he were sitting right between us, yet she tries to pretend like everything's just peachy keen in our happy home. She thinks she's protecting me, though the truth is Mom's as messed up as I am — and even worse at hiding it. Before I know it, my hands are shaking and I'm afraid I'm going to screw up my pumpkin. So I drop my knife on the table and walk over to the countertop.

I decide that two can play at this game.

"I went to a party at Teddy Baker's house yesterday," I say, waving a steaming fork full of noodles around.

"Oh, you did? How was it?"

"His mother ran off with Teddy's orthodontist. Did you know that?"

"Yes," she says, glancing at my empty chair instead of where I'm standing. "I think I heard that."

I make some *mmMMmm*ing sounds as I chew and swallow. And then I drop my fork into the sink, letting it clank against some dirty dishes. "Can I ask you something?"

She presses the tip of her knife blade into the flesh of the pumpkin and holds it steady. "Fine."

That isn't the most inviting way to change a conversational topic, but I'll take what I can get. "Do you think you'll ever date someone again?"

The skin on her forehead gets all wrinkly. "I hope you don't think for a second that I would ever date Mr. Baker."

"Eww! No." I return to my seat and take up the knife and the pumpkin again. "I'm just saying that you're divorced. So you can do whatever *you* want to do too. You know, like you said before. To me." The moment the last word drips off my lips, I tense up. I wish I could reach out and take it all back. But I can't. I've said it, for better or worse.

She takes a deep breath and slides her knife into the pumpkin. "Ruby — I'm your mother, not your girlfriend. My personal life is none of your business, and I'd appreciate it if you'd respect my privacy."

"Why are you getting all defensive?" I don't want to hurt her. I want to help her.

"Why are you purposefully trying to upset me?" she says, like I'm a traitor, the worst daughter in history.

"I'm not! I just want to talk about the way things really are." I don't get why everyone's trying so hard to shield me from living my own life. I'm about to throw down my knife and storm out of the room when I feel a pop. A pinch on the tip of my finger. Then something warm and wet. A trickle of blood rolls down the side of my pumpkin.

"Ruby!" My mom jumps up and wraps her hand tight around my finger. She hoists my hand over my head like I'm a wounded Statue of Liberty and tugs me over to the sink. "Look at what you've done." She's fumbling to open the first-aid kit with her one free hand and cursing under her breath. She says, "I shouldn't have to explain myself to you," as she swabs at the cut with a moist cotton ball.

It doesn't sting, but I can feel tears welling up in my eyes anyway. "Then stop expecting me to fill up your pathetic Saturday nights, because I have a life."

That finally does it. Mom drops the first-aid kit on the floor and takes off for her bedroom, leaving me to bandage up my finger myself.

THIRTEEN

I wasn't much help.

She was a packing machine, boxing stuff up, swirling room to room. My sadness was always in her way. I wanted to linger over the things she was wrapping up in newspaper, as if it were the last time I'd ever see them again. In a way, it was. I knew the new house would never feel like home.

To get me out of her hair, she told me to pack up the old toys in the basement for Goodwill. I doubt she would have sent me there if she'd remembered. I found it hidden at the bottom of a musty duffel bag of faded jeans and tops with big, chunky shoulder pads. An unassuming spiral notebook from the drugstore, with a red cover.

Mom only wrote in black ink and had extremely neat penmanship. It was beautiful, like calligraphy. I pressed my thumb down on the edge and watched the days of her life flicker by.

The exposed beams creaked above me. Mom walked from kitchen to bathroom to front porch. I stuffed the journal into my waistband and took off immediately for Beth's house.

At first, Beth didn't want us to read it, because she thought it might make things worse for me. Then she flipped through to the end and read the last entry, which was written before I was born, and decided it was okay.

Beth read me the journal from cover to cover during a sleepover that night. Together we analyzed facts and tidbits and potentially useful trivia. The kinds of personal things Mom would never tell me in a million years. Especially after he'd left.

She was a student at University of Akron, taking a chemistry class for nursing school. He approached her in the hallway with a cocky swagger and asked her the time. She politely pointed to the silver wristwatch he was wearing. He suggested she cut whatever class was next and go for a beer. Against her better judgment, she accepted his invitation. She was secretly thankful that her birthday was the week before, and she was now twenty-one.

That was their first date.

Mom didn't have much prior experience with guys — one boyfriend during high school, and a one-night stand where she lost her virginity to a friend's older brother a few months before she met Dad. I guess that's part of why she fell for him so fast, in just a handful of pages.

He did do some cute romantic things. Like the time he waited for her at the bus stop after her first day working at the hospital. He wore his only suit and had one of her dresses slung over his shoulder. He took her out to a fancy dinner at the big steak house up on the hill. Even Beth said that was a classy move, and I felt momentarily proud.

He proposed without a ring, in front of her two roommates, seven months later. They bought the house when Mom got pregnant.

Initially, Dad was dead set against working for Goodyear. He got by for a while, taking carpenter work, plumber emergencies, and odd jobs from the neighbors. But as Mom's belly swelled up with me, he finally relented for the sake of stability.

After his first day as a machinist on the operations floor, she had his new suit, the one he married her in, pressed. She cooked a feast modeled after his dead mother's Thanksgiving. His already-callused hands were rawer than she had ever seen, and she did him the favor of feeding him with her fork that night.

I was so confused. It seemed like they had a lot of good memories. But Beth said that journals are sometimes like photo albums. People don't put in the ugly pictures. They just keep the ones where they look pretty and happy.

I took the journal home the next morning, put it back in the duffel bag, and waited for Mom to find it. She did, later that afternoon. And while I wrapped up her collection of teakettles in newspaper, I watched out of the corner of my eye as she flipped briefly through the pages. I thought she'd get really sentimental and sad over it. I hoped she wouldn't cry. But all she did was let out a long deep sigh before stuffing it deep into a bag of trash.

FOURTEEN

I wake up obnoxiously early on Sunday morning to find a collection of hazy blue spots dotting my white ceiling. They're the kinds that appear when you look away from a bright light, even though, at seven minutes to five, my room is totally dark and so is the sky outside my window. I rub my eyes and they slowly disappear, but the memory of where I've seen them before does not.

I shuffle toward my desk in my oversized sweatpants. My desk light illuminates Friday's English exam on top of a stack of textbooks. The entire left margin is hued by blue smudges, as my palm smeared its way across the most b.s. essay ever composed on Manifestations of Guilt in *Macbeth*. This kind of inky mess incriminates any left-handed person, and my smudges are almost exact duplicates of the ones that lined the margin of Jim's letter. His sentences are blurry and broken in my memory, but I see the smudges, delicately webbed by palm prints, in sharp detail.

I head downstairs to fix myself some cereal. Mom's bedroom door is cracked open — her body is covered in a puffy white comforter and all her decorative pillows are pilled high on her dressing chair. She sleeps so close to the edge of her big mattress, not even rumpling the sheets on the other side. I close her door.

Mom must have gotten up in the middle of the night to clean up any trace of our pumpkin-carving debacle, because I walk into a spotless kitchen — knives washed and filling the silverware cup in our dish rack, trash can under our sink with a new empty bag that smells like lemon, and a Tupperware container full of seeds anchoring the center of our immaculate kitchen table. I could have cleaned up before I went to bed, but I decided against it. After all, I hadn't done anything wrong, and it had been her stupid idea anyway.

I open the front door and take a step outside. Even though the sun is rising, it's still too early to be anything but gray. The air is thick and wet, and the blacktop glistens from a night of quiet, steady rain that has stripped most of the dying leaves from their branches. Two finished jack-o'-lanterns flank me on opposite sides of the top stair. Mom carved hers and mine, following the tracings we'd made with the precision of a nurse who often wields sharp objects. Inside each, a tea light candle has burned out, leaving behind an empty aluminum shell and a charred wick.

I peel away my Band-Aid and rub my thumb gently over the long, skinny, dark scab. Her gesture could be an apology or a guilt trip. It's a toss-up either way.

A breeze kicks up in the trees, and it takes a few seconds before the chill blows against me. I pull my bare feet inside the baggy legs of my sweats, transforming them into impromptu footie pajamas. They conceal the WELCOME on our doormat, where Jim's unwelcome letter was probably left for me yesterday morning.

Right now, at the Holiday Inn, he might be sitting down to a free continental breakfast of stale pastries, bitter coffee, and watered-down orange juice, opting for a seat with a view of the lobby. Maybe he's taking a hot shower with the phone pulled close to the bathroom door, so he can hear if it rings. Or he's just lying on the bed, watching the green light on a fire alarm blink, memorizing the quiet of the empty room and wondering if it had been a mistake to look for me after all this time. These images flash in my mind in washed-out, overexposed colors, like a boring old slide presentation.

The reality is that while Jim's here now, he'll be gone again soon. He said so in his letter — he's being transferred. I can't allow some lame last-minute olive branch mess up everything else in my life. But I also know I can't obsess about it anymore. It's not good for me. I'm going to have to figure out a way to let it all go, to take control of the situation. At least until Beth finally tells me about the letter on her own accord.

And then, I get an idea.

The ride doesn't take long. There's hardly any traffic on the road this early. I fly down main streets, my bike tires purling through puddles. The wind whips against me, and I thread my thumbs through my scarf tails to protect my knuckles from the breeze.

The entrance to the Holiday Inn parking lot is a wide driveway that drops through two green grassy hills. Traffic whizzing by becomes white noise as I ride past an LED sign welcoming guests to a RUBBER TRADE SHOW WELCOME BRUNCH in the conference room. A smattering of cars fill the spots nearest to the entrance. Toward the back, near a drooping willow tree whose branches tickle puddles on the pavement, is his blue truck.

I kickstand my bike alongside it, making the truck a barrier between me and the hotel. Crouching down, I peer over the truck bed and scan the hotel windows. Most of the beige curtains are either closed for privacy or pulled wide open, vacancy style. A few are half spread, but I don't see any faces looking out. Four men in business suits loiter near the entrance, smoking cigarettes and comparing colorful ties. Leather briefcases lie next to their leather shoes. They don't notice me.

I keep low and shuffle around to the truck's front bumper and have a look at the Oregon license plate. It's actually pretty cool-looking. A huge green tree grows in the middle of six digits, and two purple mountains rise up in the distance. It's way more majestic than the red, white, and blue Ohio plate, though majestic is probably too strong a word for a license place. I let my fingers rub over the raised metal numerals and letters, leaving five winding tracks through the grime. Then I think better of it and wipe my prints away with the end of my scarf.

The front hood of the truck is dented and pinpricked with rust. The windshield is blurred by a lacquer of squashed insects from the long trip across the country. Some of the dead bugs still have a set of wings intact, but their bodies are gelatinous blobs, stuck to the glass like ooze.

I don't know why, but I pull out my Polaroid camera from my book bag and take a picture.

Then I stalk around to the passenger window and peer inside the truck. Just one look and I am flooded with memories: riding shotgun with Jim to school, or to the Giant Eagle. I was so small then, I used to press my sneakers up against the glove compartment to keep myself from sliding down the slippery gray pleather of the seats. On the seat is a blue Bic pen, dimpled by bite marks along the white plastic shaft. It's probably the one he used to write my letter. I squint at the glove compartment, trying to make out if my footprints might still be visible, but of course they're not. The bed of his truck is filled with boxes and bags full of everything that makes up his life.

I shoot a few more Polaroids, flapping each foggy white square in the brisk air until it fully develops, then sliding it carefully into the front pocket of my book bag. In one shot of his silver hubcap, you can see a funhouse reflection of me and my camera, which actually looks kind of cool. Suddenly I'm not worried about getting caught. I feel kind of brave and powerful.

Two sets of clicking high heels grow louder behind me. I look over my shoulder at a pair of businesswomen spackled in pancake makeup, watching me with suspicious, heavily mascaraed eyes. I guess I deserve it, stalking around and snapping pictures of unoccupied vehicles. After they pass me, each one turns back around to give me a last warning look.

Whatever. I should get out of here anyway.

So I climb back on my bike and picture myself saying a final good-bye to Jim as I pedal out of the parking lot. I tell him it's his fault that things are this way. I'm not yelling like I did on my birthday. Instead I'm calm and collected, which actually makes me smile with pride. Jim opens his mouth to defend himself. His lips are moving — pursed, then flat, then open in rapid succession. But no sound comes out. It's like watching a television on mute.

He doesn't have a voice because I can't remember what it sounds like.

I skid out the realization with my bike tires, and they slide against the wet pavement, nearly knocking me to the ground. He said my name that night. He did. But I can't remember the sound. I've already forgotten it.

But instead of celebrating that things might finally be going back to normal inside my head, I drop my bike and walk purposefully into the lobby, even though every one of my muscles is tightening up and telling me this is a bad idea. A man smiles at me from behind the front desk. He's helping those two women from the parking lot and I don't want to call any more attention to myself than I already have. So I pivot away from them and head toward a brass counter where three white hotel phones sit in a row. There are a lot of business types milling around with laminated name tags, and the lobby music seems like the volume is cranked up extra high to compensate. Cool sweat runs like a river down my spine as I lift the receiver. I gnaw on my hurt finger, chewing down any fingernail that might have grown overnight. Then I use it to press the barely visible numbers still scrawled in my wrist. Each one stings through the delicate scab. 4. 3. 5.

It only rings once.

"Hello?" A voice greets me. It's gravelly, probably from the smoking. Tired. Like he's slept, but not all that much. The television is on in the background. Maybe he hasn't slept at all.

He asks "Hello?" a second time, in a space of silence too small for me to have responded anyway. He sounds anxious. He wants to assume it's me, in the lobby, waiting for him. He wants this to be real.

The third time, he says my nickname. Rubes. The hairs prick up on my arms. I hang up and run back toward my bike and pedal home as fast as I can.

FIFTEEN

It's Monday morning and Katherine is cross-legged on the floor of the hallway, crying. Beth is sitting next to her, with her arm laid over Katherine's shoulder. I'm standing above them, clutching my books to my chest, and Maria is next to me, giving bold stares to the kids who slow down and try to sneak peeks of this unfolding drama. I'm the only one blushing from all the attention.

"It's pathetic," Katherine says, sniffling what sounds like large amounts of wet snot back up her nose. "My dad puts us all through the crap of him leaving Mom and moving into a new apartment, only to come back and start having *sleepovers*."

Katherine's definitely in the worst shape I've ever seen her in. And though it's nice having someone else's problems take the spotlight off my own, I'm also kind of freaked out by the whole thing. It's like watching someone literally fall apart, right in front of you.

Beth looks up at me and a tiny smile crosses her face. She's not alarmed. She's seen this all before. "Ruby, do you have any tissues?"

"No, sorry," I say. And I am. Katherine's face is a big wet mess.

Maria digs through her tote bag and pulls out a tiny packet of leopard-print Kleenex. "Here," she says, extending them with a warm smile.

Katherine takes them without saying thank you.

"Do you want us to get you something to drink?" Beth asks in a calm, even tone.

Katherine laughs. It's a weird, uncomfortable, and totally inappropriate chuckle that makes my stomach seize up. "No, I want to tell you what happened."

"Okay, okay. I just wasn't sure you were ready to talk about it right now."

Katherine rolls her eyes at Beth, as if she's totally annoying her.

I can barely stomach looking at them both, so I focus on the two boys waiting in line for the water fountain. I hate that Beth is so into Katherine's family issues, yet she didn't even bother to call me at all on Sunday, which would have been the perfect chance to talk to me about Jim's letter. It's beyond my comprehension at this point what the heck is going on inside her head.

Katherine squints her eyes and rubs her temples. "I get up to have a shower this morning and who do I see but my dad coming out of our bathroom in a towel." She empties her nose into a tissue and throws it onto the linoleum floor. "And I'm, like, 'What the hell are you doing here? You moved out, remember?' He's got this hand-in-the-cookie-jar face on and then gives me the *shhh* sign. So I push past him downstairs where Kayla and Jared are watching some stupid video for the millionth time, and they both look at me and smile and Kayla shouts, 'Daddy's back!' "

"That's awful," Beth says with a big sad sigh. She takes a clump of Katherine's hair in her hands. I can tell it isn't clean. The blond looks dull, the roots clump together near her scalp, and the ends are stringy. Beth doesn't seem to care because she starts to braid it, like she used to braid mine.

Katherine pulls a ponytail holder off her wrist and passes it backward. I can see her relax, even though my teeth are clenched so tight they start to squeak. "Meanwhile, my mom is cooking up this big breakfast in the kitchen, so I go in there and give her a piece of my mind."

"What did you say?" I ask.

Katherine looks up at me, her eyes wide and intense. "I called her a whore. And I told her this is going to stop, and if she doesn't put an end to it, I will."

My ears ring through the few seconds of silence where Maria, Beth, and I all look at each other with gaping mouths. The three of us would never, ever say something like that to our moms.

"Whoa," Maria finally says. "What did she say to that?"

"Not a word," Katherine says, smiling with a glimmer of pride. "She just kept putting bacon down in the pan. That's when I walked out."

Katherine unfurls her legs, and I notice now that she's still in her pajama bottoms. She doesn't have socks on, even though her feet are stuffed inside a pair of dirty running shoes. She's wearing a big, oversized Akron High basketball T-shirt, but as baggy as it is, I can still make out her silhouette underneath. She's not wearing a bra.

"Listen, I'm going to just cut class or something," Katherine says in a voice that now sounds extraordinarily bored. "I really don't want to be here. Look at me." She peers down at herself and her lower lip starts to tremble. She bites on it to make it stop and the pink turns to white.

Beth shakes her head. "No. Don't cut school. Trust me, that'll only make things worse. You need to keep your mind off things." She fishes her hand around in her gym bag and pulls out a black wad of fabric. "You can borrow my sports bra. It's clean."

"I think I might have a pair of jeans in my car. They might be a little long on you, but they're better than your pj's." Maria grins and Katherine manages a small but grateful smile. "I'll drop them off at your homeroom," Maria calls out as she heads toward the doors.

I don't have anything to give Katherine. So I hold out my hand to help her up from the floor. "Seriously, go to class and try to forget everything for now."

Katherine rolls onto her knees and stands up on her own. "This isn't the kind of stuff you can just forget, Ruby." She takes off down the hall, angry all over again. And I'm angry too. It's not my fault she's having family problems. Why's she all mad at me?

Beth and I head toward our homerooms. As we walk, a few kids wave and tell us that they have really cool costumes in the works for Beth's party. Beth is totally smiley and encouraging to everyone. But when we turn into an empty corridor, she snakes her arm into mine and pulls me down near her head.

"I'm really worried about Katherine," she whispers.

"Don't be," I say. "It seems like she could honestly care less about your help."

Beth shakes her head. "No. it's just that she's got a lot of anger and unresolved issues built up. The best thing we can do is help her deal with that on her own, before she does something she'll regret."

Beth's right, but it only makes me feel lonely. If she was helping me deal with everything, I probably wouldn't have gone to Jim's hotel yesterday morning. Granted, she doesn't know that I know about the letter at all . . . but still. She should know that I *should* know.

I grab hold of the straps of my book bag and make them as tight as I can. "What do you think she meant by, you know, 'put an end to it'?"

"Probably nothing. She just wants her mom to know she's upset." Beth squeezes my shoulder. "Hey, listen. I wanted to talk to you about something. I meant to call you last night, actually, but I was still trying to figure a few things out in my head before I said anything."

My heart swells up. I knew she'd say something. I knew it.

Beth takes a deep breath and closes her eyes. "There's been a big development." When she opens them, she's got on a huge smile. "Suzy surprised me with two bottles of raspberry vodka *and* a bottle of coconut rum! Can you even?"

"Oh," I whisper. My thick skin turns paper-thin. Everything hurts, even the breeze of passing students.

"So I was thinking about moving my party out of the basement. Since there's going to be a lot to drink, I figured if we were in the garage, we'd have more privacy and less chance of my parents hearing kids be all slurry or peeing in the washing machine or other stupid stuff like that. What do you think? Great idea, right? But this is going to change all the prep work I planned for the week. So could you come over after school today and help me clean out the garage? I'm reallllly going to need your help." Her voice is a little bit whiny and she sounds just like her little sister Martha when she asks for more juice. "Pleasepleaseplease?"

I open my mouth just as the warning bell rings. Beth smiles and turns away from me, I guess because she's assumed I was going to say yes anyway.

The sad part is, I was. I don't really have any other options.

SIXTEEN

I'm still in a daze as I walk through the school parking lot. Flanked by Maria and Beth, I pick up bits and pieces of their conversation about the new garage game plan. Word of the booze has traveled fast because a few kids from the drama department stop to ask if there really will be alcohol there. That reminds me, I've got to get started working on my Girl Scout badges. Maybe tonight.

We arrive at the Volvo. Maria starts the engine so we can play the radio in the parking lot. She goes around and lowers all the windows with the hand crank, letting the music escape into the air.

A voice catches in my ear, but it's not from the speakers. Someone is shouting my name. I take a few tentative steps toward the front of the car, while Maria and Beth sit on the bumper and continue chatting.

Though I hear his voice again a second before I actually see him, it doesn't make the first glimpse of him, wandering through my school parking lot, any less shocking. My book bag drops to the gravel and I fall forward, my hot and sweaty hands reacting just quick enough to prevent me from crashing into the hood.

He passes between two parked cars, right in front of me, and shouts my name with a cupped hand.

I scurry back toward Beth and Maria, who are intensely analyzing the track list of a mix CD that Davey made Maria, and how for every romantic kind of song, there's a friendship one to counterbalance it. Beth keeps shaking her head and saying "I told you so."

"Hey, Beth," I say. "We should probably get over to your house ASAP so we can get started on the garage."

He shouts my name out again, this time louder than ever. Beth stands up and cocks her head to the side. She signals Maria to turn down the radio.

"Wait! I love this song!" I plead, even though it's not a song, but an annoying commercial jingle for some kind of bladder medication. Maria ignores me and dives into the open passenger-side window. Her bare legs dangle in the air, offering a glimpse of her black boy-short underwear under the hem of her dark denim miniskirt. She quiets the volume as his voice sails over us for a fifth time.

Beth shoots me a brief look of worry before climbing up on the back bumper for a view of the parking lot. I'm scared her leather flats will slide off the chrome and that she'll fall backward, so I position myself right behind her and grab her green velvet coat. Beth's really nervous. She probably thinks it's Jim, coming to look for me. But it's not.

I peek around the side of her legs and watch him spin around in a helpless, exasperated circle. The back of his blue cardigan sweater, where the crest of Fisher Prep is stitched in gold thread between his shoulder blades, glimmers in the sunlight. He's handing out something to passing students.

"Who is *that*?" Beth asks incredulously.

"It's Charlie. The boy from the party on Saturday!" I hiss.

A glimmer of recognition flashes across Beth's face and her mouth breaks into a wide grin. She jumps down from the bumper with the flair of a dismounting gymnast. "Holy awesome!"

Charlie continues his walk down the row of parked cars next to us, his bike rolling alongside him. He makes a left at the end of the row and starts up the aisle where we are parked. I duck behind Beth and fight the smile tugging at the corners of my mouth. "What is he doing here?" I whisper into the back of her head.

"Looking for you, apparently." She raises her tiny hand up for a high five, and when I don't leap to reciprocate, she picks up my lifeless arm and slaps my hand against hers.

I shake my head. "I can't talk to him." My chest tightens with the thought of our last encounter. It's too embarrassing for me to deal with, so I push it out of my head and move to pull open one of the car doors.

"Oh, Ruby! He's totally cute," Maria coos. She pries my hand from the handle, spins me around, and rubs a wand of watermelon-flavored gloss across my lips. "And totally your type. I can tell!"

I catch a glimpse of myself in her side-view mirror. My hair looks flat and lifeless in a boring old ponytail and there's a ketchup stain on my sweatshirt from the fries I had at lunch. I peel it off and reveal my new-to-me Cleveland Browns tee. It's cute, but not enough to compensate for everything else I'm lacking. Plus, it's totally freezing outside. I should have worn my peacoat. So I put my sweatshirt back on again. "Seriously, guys. I can't do this."

"Shut up!" Beth squeals, racing to my side. She slides her thick tortoiseshell headband off her head and puts it onto mine. She splits my ponytail in half and pulls until the elastic tightens around it. Then she fluffs the scarf she knit for me up around my neck. "There. You look great." She leans into my ear and whispers, "Remember our talk in your kitchen? You do not have a problem! This is the second chance you've been waiting for!" She scratches her fingernail against the ketchup stain furiously. And then she gives me a big fat wink.

"She's over here!" Maria and Beth cry out in unison. Charlie's head perks up and looks in our direction. He climbs on his silver BMX and slowly rides over.

I think I'm going to be sick.

"Man, I never thought I'd make the ride across town in time to find you," he says, wiping some sweat off his forehead with his sleeve. I think he's a little bit embarrassed, because he's cracking his knuckles like crazy.

"Oh," I say, my eyes darting to the ground. Beth pokes me in the ribs. "So, um . . . hi."

"Hi," he says.

Maria and Beth beam huge smiles at me. I force my lips into a similar position.

"Here, you guys should have one of these. I made them up over the weekend." Charlie stuffs his hand into the pocket of his cargos and comes up with three buttons. Maria, Beth, and I each reach forward and take one. They are pink at the edges with white squares in the middle. Black letters run across everything and say: HAVE YOU SEEN RUBY? I stare at the button for a second more and then I realize: He's drawn my smile, complete with my gap teeth.

"Hey!" a voice calls out. Everyone turns to see Katherine strutting across the parking lot. She takes in Charlie with a cocked eyebrow. "Who are you?" she asks, all protective.

121

"This is a friend of Ruby's," Maria says sweetly. "Charlie."

"I was hoping we could talk." Charlie takes a step toward me. "Can I walk you home?"

"Well, I kind of had this thing planned," I stammer, turn toward Beth, and shrug my shoulders.

But she shakes her head. "No biggie. We can just do it tomorrow."

"Are you sure?"

We lock eyes. *Can I really do this?*

She shakes her head almost imperceptibly. *Yes, you can.*

The thing is, as much as I want to believe her, I don't.

"Listen," Charlie says, pressing the back of his hand against his super-red cheeks, "if walking's not your style, you can always ride on my pegs." He points at the metal bars jutting out at the center of his back tire.

He looks so cute and nice and sweet, with his rumpled school uniform. I think he even made his own tie out of blue felt. And there's really no way to decline his invitation without totally hurting his feelings. "Okay, yeah. I mean, yes. I guess so. Sure."

Katherine laughs. Both Maria and Beth elbow her. Hard.

SEVENTEEN

From the back pegs of Charlie's BMX, I lean forward and give directions out of the parking lot and onto West Market. His hunter-green baseball cap smells like salt and coconut shampoo. When I grip his shoulders, static electricity pops through my fingertips and my first instinct is to let go, but I don't. Charlie pedals forward and our bodies collectively ease into a sharp left turn. I wonder if this is what sex is like.

He wisely chooses the sidewalk over the street because traffic is unpredictable, between all the stores and parking spots and traffic lights. Unfortunately, the pavement is just as treacherous because the blocks are laid unevenly, mimicking the aftermath of an earthquake. He twists and turns his handlebars expertly and steers us clear of the biggest bumps.

The sound of his fat, rubbery tires crunching fallen leaves keeps the silence between us from being too quiet. Still, I know I should try for some conversation — if only to prove that, contrary to my recent behavior, I'm actually capable of some normalcy.

My veins knot up in fiery bundles, pumping bursts of energy and fear and giddiness through my body.

"That's where my mom got my Polaroid," I say, wagging my elbow in the direction of the camera store and remembering what brought me and Charlie together in the first place.

"Cool. Do you want to study photography or something in college?"

"I'm thinking about it," I say, even though I never really have. But I guess that would be neat. Better than studying math.

"Hey, does that shop do repairs?" Charlie tries to turn and look at me, but we almost crash into Akron Library's book drop. "Sorry." He quickly locks eyes on the path ahead.

"Umm, I'm not sure. Why?"

"I found my dad's old SLR, from his college days, when we were unpacking the Pittsburgh moving boxes. That thing is awesome, but I loaded the film wrong and messed up the advance lever. I'm afraid to take it apart to try and fix it myself. My dad will freakin' kill me if he finds out it's busted, so I've just been hiding it underneath some of his prints, hoping he doesn't decide to take it out for a sentimental spin. Thank God Akron seems to have stifled all his creativity. Anyhow, the only camera place I knew of was Best Buy, and those guys have no idea how to deal with anything that's not digital."

"SLR?" I ask.

"Single lens reflex. Don't you have one? It's like every photographer's first real camera. You can set your shutter speed, mess with the aperture, all that fun stuff. You haven't really taken a picture until you use one of those."

"Oh."

Charlie's hands strangle the handlebar grips. "I didn't mean to sound like a know-it-all. I guess I've picked that habit up from my dad. He's the kind of teacher whose lessons never really stop." He clears his throat. "So, what kinds of pictures do you like to take?"

"I don't know," I say. I could be honest and admit that I've only really had a camera for four days, but I decide against it. "Just stuff really. People and things." I'm basically describing nouns. How incredibly interesting.

"Okay . . . well, what was the last picture you took?"

A surveillance shot of my estranged father's truck. "I can't remember."

"Who's your favorite photographer?"

"You know, I never really thought about it."

"Oh." I take my hands off his shoulders to wipe the sweat onto my jeans. Charlie uses the opportunity to scratch where I've been holding him.

"I'm a fan of Annie Leibovitz," he continues. "Not the recent *People* magazine crap, but her old *Rolling Stone* covers. She shot The Kinks, The Who. I mean, all the biggest names. When bands actually had identities."

"Yeah," I say, as if I have any idea who Annie Leibovitz is, though I think it would be awesome to get paid to take pictures of rock stars. Charlie seems like he's waiting for me to say more. He keeps turning his head to the side, like he wants to make sure that I'm still on the back of his bike. "Sorry. I should have asked you who your favorite photographer was."

He leaves it be, which is a relief and also awkward. A few more blocks pass, and we turn off into quiet Akron suburbia.

The silence is back again, but different than before. We're not enjoying it together, as an old man rakes his yard, or a bunch of kids play tackle football. Instead, we're both conscious of the obtrusive emptiness. That loud kind of silence. It reminds me of hanging out with my mom, which is even more of a romantic buzz kill.

"I'm sorry if I freaked you out by just randomly showing up today," he says suddenly, weaving though a set of empty trash cans. "I just thought about you a lot this weekend."

"I wasn't freaked out."

"Right. I didn't mean freaked out like, well, *you know* . . ."

I take a deep breath and am so thankful that I am on the back of this BMX and not looking him in the face, because I just couldn't do it. Letting Charlie take me home was a mistake. For something that started off with so much promise, I can't really see this ending any way but badly.

"Just let me off at the corner," I say. "Thanks for the ride."

"Why? Where's your street?"

"Up there, on the right."

Charlie turns his handlebars and diagonals across the street, taking aim at the wall of dense, prickly bushes near the curb at the beginning of my block. "Hold on," he says with a laugh. "This'll be fun."

"Wait," I say, because we are picking up some serious speed. A car engine purrs behind us. I look back and see my mother's white Honda trailing from a distance. The ends of my ponytail whip me in the face, making my cheeks sting. I have no choice but to turn back around.

"You better hold on tighter than that," Charlie taunts as he stands up and pedals us forward with even more energy.

We are rapidly approaching death, or at least a broken rib. I scrunch the shoulders of his scratchy blue sweater into my clammy hands as Charlie suddenly hits the brakes just seconds before we crash. His back tire skids out, sending us on a whirl that makes my heart thud into my Converse.

We come to a stop, and we're both breathing heavily. I hop off the bike and let my eyes trace the long and graceful fishtail we've etched on the road. Somehow it's blacker than the black of the street. Mom slows the car and stares us down as she passes by. She doesn't wave hello or even smile, so neither do I.

"You're crazy," I tell him. Then the urge to take my camera out tugs on me and is impossible to ignore. So even though he'll probably think I'm trying too hard, I take out the Polaroid from my book bag and point it at the ground. "That's probably the longest fishtail I've ever seen." It's nearly impossible to fit the whole thing in the viewfinder, so I keep backing up on my tip-toes. Just as I snap the photo, Charlie comes up behind me, grabs my arm, and spins me around.

"You didn't want to hook up with Teddy Baker, did you, Ruby? Because when I was asking him about you, and how I could find you, he seemed to think you were . . . well, into him."

I fan my face with the Polaroid and take a step back from him. "What? No, not at all. I mean, my friend Beth was trying to . . ." I shake my head. It's not even worth getting into. "Whatever. The answer is no. I did not want to hook up with Teddy Baker."

Charlie doesn't seem appeased. He untucks his white button-down from his navy Dickies and strangles himself with his felt tie, which is covered in his homemade buttons. "Still, that wasn't very cool of me to touch your camera and pull you away from the party. I could see why that made things a little weird."

"It was fine. I mean, I was happy to get out of that basement."

"Really?" he says, with a surge of excitement. "I thought so! I mean, I was watching you for a while and I could tell by your face that you weren't having any fun there, either." He tempers himself and stares down at his feet. "Anyhow, I don't blame you at all for getting upset with me when I tried to kiss you. I shouldn't have done it like that. Not after we just barely met. I didn't even ask you if you had a boyfriend or anything."

I can't believe it. He actually thinks it was his fault that I ran away from him in tears.

I am presented with the perfect opportunity to save face. I don't have to tell him anything about why I was crying that night, or what's made me such an emotional wreck. I only have to accept his apology and we'll never speak of this again. It seems too easy. A lump bobs up in my throat. It takes a few swallows to get it down.

"Charlie, listen." I'm overcome with something. Insanity, I guess. "You didn't make me upset. It's hard to explain, but . . ." I like Charlie. I do. But I'm just not ready to go there. Especially not with someone who is still essentially a stranger. Maybe in time I can tell him what happened, or maybe I won't ever have to. But for now, I'm going to do something in the middle. "It was just some family stuff I was going through. Not anything that was caused by you." My feet take big strides toward my house, putting as much distance between us as I can.

Unfortunately, Charlie has wheels and catches up to me within a few pedals. A hand presses on my shoulder and grounds me to a stop. "Don't worry. I know what that's like."

To my surprise, he doesn't ask me a million questions. He doesn't try to figure out what's wrong with me or fix my problems. And, best of all, he doesn't leave. Charlie just rides in circles around the manhole cover in the center of the street, waiting patiently for me to catch up when I'm ready. And I know it's weird timing, but I shiver with excitement at the prospect of him possibly trying to kiss me again.

"This is my house," I say, pointing up at the stoop.

Charlie hops the curb and shows off a couple of BMX tricks for me before chucking his bike to the ground and meeting me at the bottom of my front steps. "Nice pumpkins," he says.

I reach up onto the awning and grab the spare key. "Mine's the angry-looking one."

"Hmm, I never would have guessed."

I knock into him playfully. Over Charlie's shoulder, the fuzzy outline of my mother darkens the curtains of the front window. What little confidence I have evaporates. I make eye contact with her for the briefest of seconds, and then she steps back away from the glass.

I don't have time to get my bearings. Charlie is leaning toward me, with his eyes closed, head cocked slightly to the left. It's going to happen. My first kiss! I close my eyes and wait for his lips to hit me. When they do, there's a definite spark. It might be static electricity. Or maybe something else.

I freak out over what I should be doing with my hands, but then after a few seconds, I just tuck them into my back pockets.

His go around my waist. One of his fingers, maybe the longest one, snakes up underneath the hem of my T-shirt and grazes a couple of my ribs. He's obviously kissed before. I wonder if he can tell that I haven't.

After a few seconds, I crack open one eye and check that we still have some privacy. There's a little part of me that's so glad this is happening right in my mom's face, on our front steps. Because even though I'm new at this, she could learn a thing or two from me.

EIGHTEEN

Maria's cell phone chirps the Pixies' *La La Love You*. She glances down, ignores the call, and continues our slow crawl out of the school parking lot.

The very next time she hits the brakes, she reaches into the backseat and grabs my cheeks in a kissy-face grip. "Don't think for a second I've forgotten about yesterday, Ruby." She's not angry, just whiny in a cute way. "I always spill the absolute goriest details about all my hookups to you. Remember when Rich Gilfillan had a cold and kept dripping snot on the side of my cheek when we made out on the steps of City Hall?"

"I wish I didn't," I say, pushing the words out my scrunched-up lips. Her soft hands smell like gingerbread lotion and her nails are painted a deep cranberry.

I had successfully dodged most discussion about yesterday's hookup with Charlie by devising a new hallway route, spending my lunch hour on the library computer looking up potential SLRs for myself on eBay, and letting Beth's list of remaining party plans take center stage during our after-school walk to the Volvo.

But when Maria received the call from the ring tone she's assigned to whomever she was kissing at the moment, her memory of my love life sparkles awake and leaves me nowhere to hide.

An annoying array of car horns beep impatiently behind us. Maria releases me and tsks. "You are so mean, Ruby. You never share anything with me!"

This makes me feel a little guilty. I should be better about including Maria in more of my life. But I'm not about to start that now, with Katherine riding shotgun. And especially about my first real kiss. Maria shares that stuff easily because it happens so easily for her. I'm a different, difficult story altogether.

The car lurches forward. I ease back in my seat and reapply ChapStick because my lips aren't used to being kissed and Charlie's peach-fuzz stubble wasn't as soft as it looked when we were standing forehead-to-forehead, nose-to-nose, at my front door. "You all saw the most dramatic parts. There's not much else to tell."

"Liar." Katherine's head is down in shotgun, copying someone's homework assignment into her notebook. "Beth, make her spill it. Ruby listens to everything you say."

"Shut up," I mumble.

Katherine stretches back her arm and takes dead aim at me, her middle finger acting as the crosshair. I slap her hand away kind of hard. Borderline playing, but not really. She just laughs.

Beth shrugs her shoulders. "Sorry, guys. That's about all I know myself." Her voice sounds tired and bored. Both Katherine and Maria spin back to look at us because it doesn't make any sense that Beth wouldn't know every last uncensored detail.

Last night, just as I was climbing into bed, Beth called for the scoop. She was so happy for me, but even more so for herself.

After all, she had been right — making out *was* good for me. But she was a little hurt that I hadn't raced to the phone to call her first. I explained that I had a lot of homework, and she was slightly appeased.

While she talked, my finger traced our Polaroid fishtail. The arc of the line made the perfect half to a heart shape. It was so awesome. And I was really happy. So I did tell her a few choice details, like how chewed Charlie's fingernails were and the glimpse I got of his adorable orange-and-red argyle socks when he climbed the stairs. All things considered, it would have felt weird not talking about it with her.

But then she did the Beth thing that I used to like, but now find incredibly annoying. She started giving me a few vague warnings. She said things like "Just be careful, Ruby" and "Take it slow." I was excited about Charlie, but that didn't mean I was going to do anything stupid, like instantly fall in love with him. I'm probably the last one who needs to be warned about opening up too fast.

Her little comments made me feel self-conscious. So right before we hung up, I asked Beth to keep the sordid details of my hookup to herself. I didn't want to make a big deal of it in front of Katherine and Maria. They'd already seen too much. This morning, I was mortified to see that Maria had her souvenir Ruby button pinned to a piece of leather fringe off her favorite vintage purse. If Katherine spotted that, I'd never hear the end of it.

"No problem," Beth had assured me. "You know how good I am at keeping secrets."

Including from me, it seemed.

Now, Maria adjusts her rearview mirror to get a better look at me as she makes a left onto Beth's street. "Well, can you at least tell me when you guys are seeing each other again? Did you make plans?"

"Nah. I mean, he asked what I was doing after school today, but I promised Beth I'd help her in the garage. So he told me to call him tonight."

Maria gasps and bounces up and down in her seat. The Volvo screeches to an abrupt stop a half block away from Beth's house. "You have to invite Charlie to Beth's party!"

"Oh, I don't know . . ."

"Why not? He's cute, and he obviously likes you. Seriously, I bet you a million dollars he says yes."

Katherine spits out the end of her ponytail. "Great. Ruby's going to have a date and I'm going to be stuck in the corner hanging out with Beth's little sister. Could my life get any worse?"

Beth buffs out a smudge on the window with the sleeve of her corduroy blazer, not saying anything either way.

"We'll see," I say casually. "I don't really want to take things too fast." Plus, it's not my party. I can't just hand out invitations to whomever I please.

"I think that's smart," Beth says. "You don't even really know this guy and it's not like you're anything official, like boyfriend and girlfriend."

"Not *yet* . . ." Maria trails off, in a hopeful way that makes even my pessimistic heart race. Though I'm afraid to let myself believe it, I can't help but smile. Charlie might just be my first ever boyfriend.

When I snap out of my little daydream, Beth has already left the car. I say a quick good-bye to the girls and catch up to her on the winding stone path that traces her white clapboard house.

Her mother is in the kitchen, pushing and pulling a lump of brown dough across a thick wood cutting board.

"Check her out," Beth says. "She's already cooking up party food."

Beth reaches a hand up, knocks on the window, and we both wave hello. Mrs. Miller, with shoulder-length wavy white hair and tiny green cats-eye glasses, waves back with a sticky hand. If my mom is the anti–Betty Crocker, Beth's mom is the absolute real deal. She's always preparing elaborate meals for the family, big sit-down dinners where the table is packed with different steaming dishes and everyone's shouting to pass things around. I used to eat over a lot. I used to pretend I was just another one of Beth's sisters. I had total functional-family envy.

Beth's backyard is tiny but well manicured, even in the fall. Somehow the lawn is still green and thick, and there's not a single dead leaf to be found anywhere. The border of the yard is edged with a low cherrywood fence. Chubby bright purple and red mums sprout up from the moist, dark soil. It could almost pass for spring, if not for the fact that it's only four o'clock and the sun has almost completely set.

A two-car garage sits at the end of the driveway, in the far corner of the property. It matches the main house perfectly, with crisp white siding and green window shutters. Wooden flower boxes hang from the windows, filled with tiny gourds and pumpkins.

This used to be our clubhouse when we were younger — a place where Beth and I would play when it rained, or when we stole something from Suzy, like a curling iron, and wanted to fool around with it without getting caught. Or, later on, when I was upset and too embarrassed to be seen by anyone but her. The last time I was in here, I think I was twelve.

Beth unlocks the side door and pulls it open. I follow her into the cool, dark room, moving slowly while my eyes adjust to the lack of light. She takes a few steps into the center, tripping on something along the way, and waves her hand over her head until she swats a dangling cord. A single naked bulb flickers to life above our heads, illuminating an absolute disaster area.

The garage is full of stuff. Almost every available inch is occupied by electric tools, gardening accessories, or backyard toys. There's an old refrigerator humming in the corner. That will come in handy, but the space is looking totally rough and nowhere near party-ready.

Beth pouts and crosses her arms. "We're never going to get this place cleaned up in time. I should have started working on this yesterday, but I didn't want to do it alone!" She collapses onto an old Strawberry Shortcake Big Wheel with peeling, weathered decals.

I won't let myself feel guilty about blowing off our plans for Charlie, because Beth had said it was no big deal. I stoop to pick up a hula hoop, a basketball, a garden hose, and a power drill. "It's going to be fine," I assure her.

"But I've got to clean *and* decorate! And it's freaking Tuesday already! Maybe we should just go back to the original plan and have the party in the basement like always. It's just — I don't want to get caught with that alcohol. That would totally ruin my birthday."

I spin and take in the whole garage. It *is* a mess, but the space needs more picking up random junk than a real thorough cleanup job. "Listen, it's definitely smarter to party in here than in the basement. It's too easy to get caught inside your house." I shrug off my book bag and hang it, along with my scarf, from Beth's bicycle handlebar. "I say we pick up as much as we can for the next hour and then you decorate while I finish tidying up. My mom's not going to be home until late tonight anyhow. I'll stay with you until it's done."

Beth stands back up, divides her hair into two messy little buns, and smiles. "Thanks for helping me, Ruby."

"Shut up," I tell her. After all, what am I going to do? Beth is still my best friend. And regardless of all the craziness going on, I've got a lot of friendship debt to pay back.

We work in between spurts of conversation about how to best set up the room — where the stereo should be (on her dad's work-table), where to send people to pee (her neighbors' bushes), and places for people to sit down if they want (plastic lawn furniture, an old beanbag chair, a garden bench). We drag out the biggest stuff, like the bicycles and the plastic snowmen and the lawn mower, and hide it behind the garage for the time being. It only takes us a few trips before the space really opens up.

We are inspired and hungry after an hour. Beth disappears into the house to get us some snacks and to bring in her collection of decorations from parties past. Meanwhile, I stack a few of her father's plastic planters into each other and stick them underneath his workbench. That's when I knock something over. I reach deep into the darkness and pick it up.

It's a heavy, glass mason jar filed with a bubbly, opaque oily mixture. I hold it up to the light and see the remains of a soggy Q-tip sink to the bottom. My knees go weak.

It's one of the batches of bathroom poison we created to use on Jim. The idea was that, if he ever tried to come back, I'd pour a few glugs of this into his morning coffee.

Without a second thought, I grab my camera from my book bag and set up a shot with the jar poised on the edge of her father's worktable. I take a big step back and inch slightly to the left, so that the raw bulb hangs in the background. It makes the whole shot look that much more depressing.

"Ruby," Beth says flatly. I look over my shoulder at her in the doorway, holding two tall glasses of apple cider and a plate of cookies. "What are you doing? Why would you want a picture of *that*?"

"I don't know," I say. But I turn away from her and take the photo anyway.

Beth sets down the tray and picks up the poison, cupping it carefully with both hands. "I don't understand you. Do you *want* to make yourself upset?"

"No." It's not like I went looking for the jar. I just happened to find it. I cross the room and bury the photo and my camera deep in my book bag.

"Well, what is it, then?" Beth asks, following me. She sets the jar down and gives my shoulder a supportive squeeze. "You can't be mad at yourself for this!"

"I'm not mad at myself," I say. I pick up the jar and hurl it into a nearby trash can. The weight sends it ripping through the layers of dead leaves and brittle newspaper until it thuds at the bottom of the can, puffing up a cloud of dust. "But you know, maybe I wouldn't have had to go through all this if my mom and I could have just talked a bit more about what happened. I mean, don't you think it's a little weird we've never discussed him? At all? Even to this day, after he randomly shows up?"

Beth's face is blank. Totally emotionless. Which is crazy to me. I mean, this whole secret-letter business wouldn't even be a thing to hide if everything could have just been out in the open from the start. Beth should get it. She should blame my mom too. Maybe I'm not explaining myself enough, so I struggle to string more words together.

"I didn't even tell you that she was hiding behind the curtains, watching me kiss Charlie yesterday. That was after we'd had a fight about her moving on and trying to date someone else. It doesn't get more messed up than that."

Beth's shoulders rise and fall with even, measured breaths. "I've never heard you talk like this about your mom," she says softly. Definitely disappointed.

"I'm just saying, you know, that she could have made it easier on me if she wasn't so closed off."

"Ruby, your mom's put up walls to protect herself. Like you did."

I throw my hands up in the air. "But we don't need to have walls from each other! We're supposed to be in this together." I stare at her. Hard.

"I'm not taking sides, Ruby. Even though I always have your side." Beth says this with a tiny smile. "I just think it's probably weird for her to talk about it *now*. I mean, so much time has passed."

"I don't understand," I say. I really don't. I don't understand anything.

Beth shifts her eyes onto a knot of fake spiderwebs that need untangling. "Look. All I am saying is that if your mom still isn't ready to deal with things, you can't force her. There were times I'd get super frustrated with you. But I didn't say anything. I had to let you work it out on your own."

Beth has a point. You can't force someone to get over something, as much as you want them to. You just have to let them work it out on their own. But if my best friend really did believe what she was saying, she'd have given me the letter from Jim instead of stealing it. She would have let me deal with it on my own, in my own way, and supported me no matter what. And that, as much as I don't want to admit it, makes her whole speech pretty much a crock.

NINETEEN

"Wow," Beth says, drawing out the vowel sound with all the breath left in her lungs. She leans over the edge of the loft. "I never thought we'd be able to top the basement, but the garage looks freakin' amazing!"

I grit my teeth, tear the roll of yellow caution tape, and tie the last of three sagging streamers that form a crude and extremely unsafe railing. Then I inch carefully to the edge of the plywood and peer over my toes. Countless lit candles flicker an eerie light on our progress from the last five hours.

A toothy, silver power saw on her dad's workbench digs violently into a plastic hand. A huge pumpkin is punctured by a million nails. A Christmas reindeer has a sparkly gunshot wound to the abdomen, made from Elmer's glue and red glitter, and black electrical tape Xs over his eyes. Plugged in, he's a glowing corpse. Some old red paint splatters a bloody outline for the dance floor and five white-chalk outlines of my "dead" body freeze-dance on the concrete.

My arms tingle with goose bumps, because it really does look awesome.

Our hard work was also a distraction from the earlier tension. We cleaned, then brainstormed decorating ideas and made things, both of us keeping our minds on the tasks at hand or the music on the radio. At least, I tried my best to.

But with every cool idea we had for the party, I kind of wished that Charlie could see what we were doing. I knew he'd be impressed, considering the lameness of those Fisher Prep socials. Maybe, if things were still all right between us by the end of the week, I'd ask Beth if I could invite him.

Still, I don't really like the idea of Charlie creeping into my mind so often, so soon. I don't want to memorize his freckles or collect a bunch of his adorable buttons that I'd just have to throw away if things didn't work out.

Maybe I won't call him tonight, even though he asked me to.

"Hey," Beth says, snapping her fingers near the tip of my nose. "Don't think so much. You'll hurt yourself."

I laugh weakly at that, and Beth echoes with a hollow chuckle of her own. Then a deafening silence suffocates us.

We climb down the rickety wooden ladder, her first, me second. When I get to the bottom, Beth's mouth opens and closes, like a lawn mower that needs its cord pulled a few times before it can start up.

But the last thing I want to do is be here longer than I have to. I feel like I'm on the verge of totally losing it with Beth; but as upset as I am about everything, I don't want that to happen. It's just going to make things worse. So I plaster on a smile and beat her to the punch. "I guess I should take off, before I pass out cold and end up sleeping on the floor."

"Oh," she says, and matches my phony smile. "Okay."

While I put on my peacoat, Beth disappears into the house and returns with a bag of felt scraps she's swiped from her mom's sewing room. They're for me to make Girl Scout badges with.

I hesitate taking them from her outstretched arm. "But what if your mom needs them for something?"

"Shut up," Beth says, swatting me with the bag, so I take them and follow her into the yard. The sky is dark blue and littered with stars. "Ooh. And I also printed out some original Scout badges from the Internet. So you can copy them."

"Oh. Thanks." My stomach growls audibly.

"You sure you don't want some leftover pizza? My mom ordered extra for you."

Over Beth's shoulder, I watch through the big bay window as her family clears the dinner table assembly style — her mom with the plates, her younger sister Martha collecting the silverware, followed by Mr. Miller stacking the cups. Everyone is smiling, like it's fun to do chores or something. That's part of the reason I was over here so much when I was growing up. But something about tonight feels different and empty in a way that's bigger than just my belly.

I take a couple of backward steps away from her and paw around behind me for the fence gate until the wood scrapes my hand. "Thanks, but I better get back home." Beth's mouth wrinkles up. I turn away and speed walk toward the street.

I guess it's just hard sometimes to have a happy, functional family like Beth's in my face, when all I have is a mess that my mom can't talk about and my best friend doesn't really understand. I don't even understand it. My knees bump into the plastic bag as I walk, sending it spinning in circles, tightening around my wrist like a noose. My fingertips throb red.

It doesn't make sense to rush back to an empty house with nothing but old birthday ziti in the refrigerator. I check my wallet. Skimping a bit on lunch every day usually nets me about an extra ten dollars a week. I've got twenty on me — enough for a comfort-food feast of epic proportions, courtesy of Dodie's 24-hour breakfast menu. I head in that direction and try to replace my discontent with the thought of pancakes.

I don't know why I'm letting all this get to me right now anyway. It's stupid. My mom is going to do what she wants, and if she's hell-bent on pining away for Jim, then whatever. Beth is right. There's really nothing I can do about it.

But there's just a part of me that can't believe how easy Beth seems to lie to me, again and again and again. I wonder if it's something she's struggling with. Is it hard for her? If I were holding in a secret that big, I'd have it painted all over my face. It'd be really tough to keep it from her. Probably even impossible.

When I arrive at Dodie's, the sight inside is anything but a comforting one. The late-night dinner crowd is in full effect. Everyone has silver hair, if they have hair at all. They dine solo across from empty chairs, the living halves of partially deceased couples, slowly sipping their coffee, counting out pennies from their pockets to pay their bills, and stuffing those same pockets back up with sugar packets and creamers and little tubs of jelly.

There's something so lonely and unavoidable about it. I take out my camera and point it though the window. In a strange way, I'm discovering that things become easier to look at through my viewfinder. But I can't get a good shot. The glare from the

Highland movie theater marquee next door shimmers off the glass and makes it hard to see.

I cup my hand to shield away the blurry reflection of the people leaving the eight o'clock show. There's only a handful. The Highland isn't popular, especially with the cushy mega-plexes that are just across the highway. This one is small, the uncomfortable seats make your butt cheeks fall asleep and tingle, and they always play an old ENJOY THE SHOW reel with cheesy lasers and weird robotic music from a 1970s exercise video. That's actually something I like. Every time I go with Beth and Maria, we pretend to dodge the lasers or fake *oòh* and *aah* at the screen.

I notice one straggler leaving, lingering behind the rest of the crowd. He walks toward a blue truck parked across the street.

Oh my God.

I duck into the shadowy doorway of Dodie's, pull up the hood of my sweatshirt, and watch. Jim unlocks the door of the truck and removes what looks like a small cardboard box the size of a loaf of bread. After feeding the parking meter some change, he walks in the direction of where I live, with that box tucked under his arm.

It's like I've got magnets in my pockets or something, the way my body just follows him without even thinking. I keep a wide distance between us. I glide from tree to parked car to mailbox to trash can, like some kind of burglar. I curse myself repeatedly for ever going to his dumb hotel and calling him up on the lobby phone. That only encouraged him, made him think I wanted to see him. What a stupid, stupid move.

At first I think Jim is lost. He's walking in long, loping strides, and he keeps looking around at the other houses and into the sky, like he's hoping for a landmark to help him figure out just where he is. But after a few blocks, he takes a turn that makes me feel sick to my stomach. He knows exactly where he's going. To Rose Lane, to our old house.

When he gets there, he stands across the street. I look down at my feet, afraid of how it might make me feel to watch this. But eventually I lift my chin. A few lights are on in the house, and the windows flicker with the shadows of people moving around upstairs. Smoke curls out of the chimney. I shiver.

Dad walks right up to the house. He doesn't use the path, just trudges up the lawn. I can hardly breathe. He wedges himself between two shrubs and rubs his hands over the new siding, which I notice now is blue instead of the peeling white it used to be when we lived there. The repairs he never made.

I glance around. If someone sees him here, they'd definitely call the cops. But the street is eerily quiet. He finally walks away and makes a left.

After fifteen minutes and a few wrong turns, he finds my street. His pace was slow before, but now it gets even more lumbering. Like he has to convince himself of every step forward.

I turn the corner and duck for cover behind a big green bush in a neighbor's yard. My house looms on the other side, catty-corner across the street. The wet ground seeps through the knees of my already dirty jeans. I crack spindly branches aside and make a little peephole through the yellow, dying leaves.

When he gets to my front door, he stands still for a while and lights up a cigar. The smoke catches on the breeze and blows in my direction. With every inhale, he shifts his weight. Thank God our driveway is empty and Mom has a late shift at work. He takes in the house until he is interrupted by a deep guttural cough that I can hear even from across the street. He gasps for breath and his shoulders shake. Then he approaches the top step, sets the box he's been carrying on the welcome mat, and starts walking back down the middle of our street. I close up the bushes and pray for invisibility as he walks past where I'm hiding. On the way, he drops his lit cigar stub. Half-smoked, it burns red against the street. I track him, not breathing, not even blinking, until he turns the corner and disappears.

My mom will be home any minute. I stand up and sprint across the street, up the stairs, and skid to a stop at the cardboard box. It has my name on it, traced over and over and over again in that blue Bic pen. Beth isn't around to intercept it this time, to protect me from what might be inside. It's here, just for me. And I am so afraid.

I think for a second about throwing it into one of the trash cans that sit just to my right. But instead, I take one last cautious look over my shoulder, reach up for the spare key, and take the box in my shaking hands.

After locking my bedroom door, I use a dirty fork sitting on my desk to cut through the tape. I peel back the cardboard flaps.

There are a bunch of old photos inside. The prints are perfect squares, rimmed with a white scalloped border. Some are of Jim, some are of him and Mom. Some are of my mom with a baby bump, smiling. Mom's hair is really long, hanging down over her boobs like a mermaid. Jim is struggling to grow a beard. He looks rugged and handsome. His hands are dirty in some shots, shoved deep in his pockets in others. They don't look in love. They just look young.

The rest of the stuff in the box is pretty random. Jim's old Goodyear company ID, a few badges from the forestry service, a pocketknife that's rusted closed.

There's no note. No explanation.

He's delivered his best garage-sale items. He expects me to rummage through a box of old junk to figure out who exactly he is. This isn't the retro stuff I like, the vintage goods to make up stories for. I know how this one ends. Before I can stop myself, I hurl the entire box against my wall, sending the contents fluttering everywhere.

A twinkle grabs my attention. A silver watch clouded by smoky gray tarnish lies a few feet away. I bend over, pick it up, and try to clasp it to my wrist. But the latch is broken. So I just hold it there and try to think for a second.

TWENTY

It was our routine.

First, Dad would drive us to the Giant Eagle and we'd head straight for the frozen-food aisle. He loved Stouffer's brand macaroni and cheese in the bright orange boxes. He said it wasn't as good as Mom's homemade, but he'd still scrape the plastic clean with his fork and, when he thought I wasn't looking, his tongue. I'd get the French bread pizza, usually pepperoni. Then we'd stop off at the newspaper shop and buy a couple lottery tickets.

After baking our meals side-by-side in the oven, we'd eat in front of the television and hang out until the nine o'clock drawing came on. My dad loved the lottery. He'd play my birthday and Mom's, and his mother's — the grandmother who died before I was born. We'd had a deal that if he ever won, I'd get to stay up an extra hour. If he lost, I had to go right to bed. He always let me hold the pink paper tickets.

Unfortunately, Dad usually lost.

But on one particular night, the lottery lady counted out my mother's birthday. Dad and I whooped and hollered — he'd won one hundred and thirty-five dollars. And I won an extra hour before bedtime, so I stayed put on the couch.

Sometime later, I started to doze off. But instead of bringing me upstairs. Dad got me a blanket. "Mom is going to be so excited to know she's lucky," he said. "We'll stay up and surprise her."

"Okay," I said. And then I fell back asleep.

I woke up again. The whole house was dark, the television was off. I had snuggled onto my dad's arm, but he kept shaking, which was what woke me up. Not on purpose to tell me to go to bed, or because he was cold. He kept lifting up his arm to check his silver watch.

"What are you doing?" I asked through a yawn.

He looked at his watch again. "You should go to bed."

I shook my head.

He sighed. "Do you want me to show you how to tell time?"

This time I nodded my head up and down.

When the lesson was over, the little hand of the silver watch was on the three. The big hand was on the twelve. And my mom still wasn't home from the hospital.

TWENTY-ONE

I'm sitting Indian-style on the floor of my closet, hiding from the land-mine field that my life has become. There are little explosives hidden all around me and I don't know where it's safe to step. I'm afraid of triggering something. A picture, a trinket, someone else's happiness. Everything feels dangerous.

The closet is a huge paper bag, helping me not to hyperventilate. I'm trying to breathe slowly, in even, measured breaths. The portable phone sits in my lap, mocking me while I run through the short list of people I can't talk to about how I'm feeling.

Suddenly, it rings. I actually flinch.

"You didn't call, like you said you would," Charlie says instead of hello.

"Sorry," I say, and smooth my hair off my forehead. The disappointment in his voice is slightly comforting. "Anyhow, I was going to call you later, after I finished this thing I'm doing."

"It's past midnight, you know."

Uh-oh. How long have I been sitting in here? And if it's really that late, my mom is going to freak out that I'm getting phone calls. "Hold on a second," I whisper.

"Okay," he whispers back.

I stick my head outside the closet into my dark bedroom. I can hear the water rushing through the pipes overhead. I duck back inside and shut the door again.

"I didn't get you in trouble, did I?"

"No, my mom's in the shower. But you can't call here this late."

"So what are you doing that you couldn't call me?"

I look above at the hems of T-shirts hanging over my head. "I'm in my closet."

"Oh." Charlie takes a deep breath. "Wait. You're not talking metaphorically, are you? Because that's going to make me way less excited about finally kissing you."

I can't help but laugh. "No, Charlie. I mean, I'm literally sitting on the floor of my closet." I shift my weight and pull out a red rubber wellie from underneath my butt and toss it aside.

"What are you doing in there?"

"Just sitting in the dark."

"Thinking?"

"Trying not to think, actually."

"Got it," he says, and starts to cough. It sounds fake. "I think you need to try harder."

"What do you mean?"

"Well, you keep sighing these little sad sighs. Like, right before you speak. Nearly every time. Which makes me think that you're actually thinking about whatever you're trying not to think about."

There's a long silence. I hold my breath and pray that he's not going to try and make me have a big discussion right now.

"Can you cut class tomorrow?" he asks, hopeful. "My dad's teaching some master screen-printing class at Kent State, which will be incredibly pretentious but interesting. I was going to play hooky and go along to check out the class and see their photography collection. They've got prints by everyone there. Ansel Adams, Diane Arbus — "

"Diane Arbus?" I perk up and try to place the name. It was Maria who mentioned her, when I was about to snap that funny picture of the boys wrestling. "My friend said my pictures reminded her of Diane Arbus."

"Really? That's a huge compliment. Her work can be so funny, but also totally sad and . . . I don't know. It's pretty amazing all the feelings she can elicit from a single picture." He pauses, I can hear him breathing. Then he shifts his phone from ear to ear. "So you think you might want to get out of Akron for a day and check it out with me?"

That's exactly what I want. "Yeah, okay."

"Great," Charlie says, his smile almost audible. "We'll pick you up at nine-thirty. Make sure you bring your camera."

TWENTY-TWO

It's not easy to convince a nurse that you're sick when you really just want to cut school to hang out with your almost-boyfriend. But I'm trying really hard.

"I felt pretty crappy last night," I say in my best sore-throat voice, the covers pulled all the way up to my chin. "I didn't even eat dinner." That's actually true, but I toss in a fake cough for good measure.

Mom sits on the corner of my bed, just kind of staring at me. She's in her scrubs again, about to head back to the hospital. She's been working double shifts whenever possible, to help pad our savings. "You threw up in the shower this morning?" she asks quietly.

"Just, like, a little bit. I was dry-heaving and dizzy and yeah. But my stomach was pretty much empty, so it wasn't a big spew." My head drops back into the pillow and I close my eyes like I'm weak.

A muffled chime interrupts my performance. I keep my eyes closed and swallow hard.

"What's that?" Mom asks, rising off the bed and walking toward my closet. "Is that the cordless? Why is our phone in your closet?"

After hanging up with Charlie, I had cleaned up Jim's box of crap as quickly as I could, trying not to look at any of it too closely. Then I threw it, and all the rest of my Polaroids, in the back of my closet for safekeeping. Apparently I forgot to take the phone back out with me.

The closet door creaks open. "Oh, Ruby. This is a disaster area." She huffs and puffs, kicking some stuff around, searching for the ringing phone.

My mom would probably die if she found that box. I could try to explain that it wasn't something I'd asked for, that I didn't have anything to do with its arrival. But I don't think that would help much. Whatever was left of her broken heart would shatter and I'd be responsible.

Finally, the ring sounds a bit louder. The phone's been safely unearthed. I open my eyes the littlest bit and watch my mom bend over and click the receiver on.

"Hello?" Mom says. "Oh, hi, Beth. She's right here. Hold on one second." She walks the phone over to me, sits down on the corner of my bed, and puts the back of her hand against my forehead.

"Hey," I say, sitting up slowly.

"Maria just beeped outside my house. We're on our way over."

"I don't think I'm going to school today," I say, and make eye contact with my mom. She doesn't disagree with me. I remind myself not to smile.

"Are you okay?" Beth sounds genuinely worried. "You know, I thought something was up with you yesterday. I shouldn't have kept you out in that cold garage for so long."

Wow. I'm getting out of Akron and have a justifiable excuse for acting weird at Beth's house yesterday. Cutting school with Charlie is already awesome. "It wasn't your fault."

"God, I'd feel terrible if you were too sick to come to my party. Like, I might as well not have it at all."

I roll my eyes. Even though she's my best friend, there's no way anything could come between Beth and her party. "I'm sure I'll be better by Friday, probably even tomorrow. I just need to take it easy and relax today."

Beth offers to collect my homework assignments. I tell her to hold on, and repeat that information to my mom. If she even suspected for a second that I was faking, the fact that Beth will be at school without me pretty much guarantees that I'm not up to any trouble. And I don't feel the littlest bit guilty about lying to Beth. In fact, it might help things between us, level the playing field somewhat.

Even though she's probably still skeptical, Mom calls the school secretary and tells her I won't be coming in. Before she leaves for the hospital, she fixes me some dry toast, which I promise to try and eat when the room stops spinning.

That's definitely overkill at this point. But whatever.

As soon as Mom leaves, I leap out of bed and throw together an outfit. I don't want to look dressed up, but I want to fit in on a college campus. And look cute too, I guess. So I put on my borderline-disgustingly-dirty Levi's and a long-sleeved white T-shirt with a tiny green-apple print that actually makes me look like I have boobs. I pair that with a fuzzy navy cardigan with pretty pearl buttons and my navy New Balances. I put on the chocolate-colored leather belt that says GRANDPA in tan stitching across the back, because I bet Charlie will find that funny. We get each other like that.

Because I stayed in bed for a while after my shower, my long hair's doing that wavy thing again, which I'm pretty happy about. But my face looks really plain and boring.

I head downstairs and tiptoe into my mother's bedroom, even though I know she's gone and I could stomp and scream if I wanted to. Her bed is made as usual, overflowing with about twenty different throw pillows in colors that coordinate to her comforter just so. Her oak dresser is topped with delicate perfume bottles and pastel lotions and baskets of other girly products that are foreign to me. After moving a few things around, I find the one tube of shimmery lip gloss that she had bought for me awhile back, only to repossess a few weeks later when she figured I'd never wear it. I smear it on and slide the tube into my pocket.

A horn beeps outside my house and catches me off guard. It's only nine-fifteen, but I peer through Mom's lace curtains and see that Charlie and his dad are parked outside. I sprint back upstairs, throw my camera and my last pack of Polaroid film into my book bag, and fly out of the door with my gray peacoat over my arm and my scarf wrapped around my neck. Charlie smiles at me the whole way down the stairs. I wipe some extra lip gloss from the corners of my mouth as inconspicuously as I can.

"Hey," I say quietly as I slide into the backseat.

"Hi," Charlie says, turning around from the front seat. He looks cuter than ever in dark jeans and a V-neck sweater that's the color of oatmeal. He's got a sky-blue T-shirt peeking out with a dark blue splotchy pattern I can't quite recognize. And there's a white thermal underneath that too. I'm afraid he might be too cold to walk around and explore the campus, but then I spot a black ski jacket folded up on the seat next to me.

"This is Ruby," Charlie says to his father.

His father doesn't say anything to me. He just turns up NPR and takes off down the street once I'm buckled up.

We sit in silence on the way out of Akron, except for when Charlie's dad curses the traffic and the bad drivers and the mini-malls under his breath. He's dressed in tones of black and gray. His hair is white and his glasses are clear plastic. There are a few colorful flecks of paint on the lenses, and one small smear of blue behind his ear.

"Did you pack my test sheets?" Charlie's dad says suddenly, as he turns to face his son in an almost accusing way. His profile is sharp and pointy. I don't think he looks like Charlie too much. I guess Charlie looks like his mom.

"Yeah. And the inks you mixed last night. Everything's in the trunk."

"What about the screens I burned?"

"In the trunk." Charlie turns and smiles at me.

His father is silent again for a few minutes. "This class is going to be terrible," he says. He glances at me in his rearview mirror and scratches his neck.

"You know, Ruby, my dad's class was filled in fifteen minutes. Some of the regular professors are even taking it."

His dad bites on his finger. "And they will all be disappointed. Carnegie-Mellon might as well have cut off my arms. I can't work anymore. This city is so . . . *uninspired*."

"It's definitely not Pittsburgh," Charlie says. "I miss it there too." He snakes his arm through a gap in his seat and squeezes my knee. "But Akron has some good things about it."

My entire body heats up. I crack the window.

His dad gives a snarky laugh. "Try telling that to your mother, and maybe then she'll come home from MacDowell."

"That's an artists' colony in New Hampshire," Charlie explains to me. "She's working on her sculptures there for a few months in some private cabin in the woods."

"Cool," I say.

"Because she hates it here too," his dad adds. "Even more than me, if you can imagine that!"

"Oh," I say, because . . . I have no idea how to answer that.

"Hey! I have something to show you." Charlie rummages around in the bag on his lap. "I made this at the art camp I was telling you about, when I was a kid."

He hands me a stack of Polaroids. Each has two holes punched through the thick white border and the pile is threaded tightly with a thick red string. The first picture is of a young Charlie, probably about ten years old. He's in a tie-dyed T-shirt and khaki skater shorts, and he has long messy brown hair. He's perched at the top of a playground slide.

"What is this? A photo album?"

"Nope," he says with a grin. "It's a flip book."

I steady my thumb on the edge of the pictures and press down. Suddenly, the image of Charlie springs to life, flickering as he cascades down the slide, stands up, and throws his hands up in celebration. It's the coolest thing I've ever seen.

"I have to make one of these for a friend of mine," I say, thinking of Beth's birthday present. It's just perfect for her. A little sadness tries to creep into my mind but I won't let it.

"We can do that today, while we're walking around Kent."

"Charlie, I told you a hundred times I'm going to need you to set up my lab," his dad barks.

But Charlie doesn't get upset or react, even though his father is being a pretty big jerk. He's just nice and patient, like he is with me. "Yeah, definitely, Dad. We'll do that first and check out the campus after you're all settled in your studio. Sound good to you, Ruby?" This time, he extends his hand up to me for a high five.

I slap him back and smile larger than I have in forever as Akron fades away behind me in the distance.

TWENTY-THREE

As if I couldn't have guessed, Charlie's dad acts like a total spaz once we arrive on the Kent campus. We park in the faculty section, near the Fine Arts building. After turning off the car, he sits still for a while, his hands gripping the wheel. I'm kind of afraid to move or make any noise, but Charlie gets out of the car like it's no big deal, so I do too.

Charlie and I unload the trunk while his dad gets it together. I honestly don't mind the weirdness. We have a good time piling up each other's arms with more crap than we could ever possibly carry in a comfortable way. A little bit of green ink, left on one of the screens, smears across my favorite jeans and I don't even care.

When we get up to the printing studio, I'm pretty blown away. The space is huge and empty and white, with a bunch of wooden workstations and a huge pushpin wall to display every-one's work. Charlie carefully unfurls big pieces of beige paper from the cardboard tubes. His dad's prints are amazing. Most of them are enormous wall-sized landscapes, built up with hun-dreds of passes of ink done over and over and over with different colors, in tiny little shapes to make one huge picture. I hold up one corner while he tacks the other with a pushpin and take a closer look. It's pretty insane. Some of them are so detailed, they look like photographs.

Charlie explains that it can take his dad hundreds of passes to complete one piece of art. And if the paper slides askew just the teensiest bit, then the whole print is ruined. When his dad is working in his home studio, Charlie's not even supposed to walk around downstairs, for fear the vibrations might shift a screen or screw something up. It sounds like life at home is stressful for him too.

Charlie's dad trudges into the room after us and sits on a metal stool near one of the big picture windows. He stares down at the campus below, taking quick small sips from a sleek metal thermos. I think he might throw up.

"Is he okay?" I whisper to Charlie as he arranges tubes of paint on a desk in an order I don't really understand but seems very intentional.

"Yeah, he's fine." He looks up at me and rolls his eyes. "Sorry if this isn't fun, but I just have to finish up a few things and then we can go exploring."

I just smile. I don't want to rush him.

After ten more minutes of arranging, and another ten of Charlie whispering things to his dad as his students and a few adults file in, we head to the elevator and press the ground level. Students get on and off during our ride to the ground floor. I wonder if they think we are college students too.

Charlie presses something into my hand. It's a blue button that says I DON'T GO HERE in electric-yellow type. I laugh while he pins the same one to his sweater and rustles his hands through his majorly messy hair. Then, he rustles mine.

We go for a slow walk outside. The wind is blowing crazy hard against us. Charlie loops his arm into mine so we can both keep our hands stuffed in our pockets for warmth.

"Thanks for all your help in there," he says.

"No problem," I say. "Your dad's stuff is amazing. He really doesn't need to be nervous."

"Yeah, I know. He's just been a little off since the whole Pittsburgh incident."

I don't know if I should press Charlie for details. So I just turn a little to the side and pretend like I'm really interested in the group of kids who are cuddled around a laptop underneath a tree on a big plaid blanket.

"You can ask me what it is I'm talking about. I mean, if you're interested in, you know, knowing."

He sounds a little hurt at having to extend the invitation, but I was only trying to protect his feelings. "Ah, okay. What are you talking about?"

"He lost his job. Well, I guess you could say that he didn't get the promotion he was looking for, so he quit. He thought the director would chase after him, but he didn't. So his pride was really wounded, because my dad thinks he's hot shit. Which he kind of is, but whatever. So when he got the chance to teach a few master's classes at Kent, we up and moved. And he's been miserable ever since."

"Wow."

"Yeah. The best way to deal with him is to treat him like a kid. Helping him, telling him he's doing a great job, convincing him that his stuff is still innovative and whatever else. I think most artists are really insecure. I mean, I know I am."

"Come on. You?"

"Seriously. You should have seen me last night, trying to figure out if I had the guts to call you."

I push my hair off my shoulder in an attempt to hide my smile. "I'm definitely the most insecure person I know."

"Well, you're an artist, so I guess that makes sense."

I kick around a few pebbles. "I don't think it's that exactly."

"I can tell the way you look at stuff. You're definitely an artist, whether or not you know it yet." He smiles at me.

I take out my camera, and Charlie helps me make a photo flip book, which I guess I'll give to Beth for her birthday. Since she always complains that I never smile like a normal person, we take about ten photos as I go from a tight-lipped, plain face to a big, normal grin.

Then we go and get vegan sloppy joes at this crazy place called Zephyr's. I'm a little afraid of fake meat, being that I'm a huge fan of the breakfast sausage at Dodie's, but it actually tastes good. Not quite like meat, but still yummy. Charlie saves me some of his hero to feed to the weird black squirrels Kent has running all over campus.

We follow some flyers and enter a gallery for the fashion school. They have a whole bunch of costumes on display in glass cases from the fibers majors. I wonder if Beth knows you can major in fibers. I certainly didn't.

"What are you going to be for Halloween?" Charlie asks, checking out one insane butterfly costume made completely out of woven labels from Mountain Dew bottles.

"I found an old Girl Scout uniform at the thrift store. But I e to make my own badges."

ute," he says. "What kind of badges?"

I think back to the printout Beth had placed in the bag of felt scraps. "Probably classic stuff, like birdhouses and rainbows and a guitar."

Charlie stops walking and puts both his hands on my shoulders. "Wait. You know how to play guitar?"

"No," I say, shrugging him off to get a better look at a knight's suit of armor, knit entirely with Christmas tinsel. "That's just one of the badges." Sometimes I think I disappoint Charlie, in a way. Like he's expecting me to be cooler than I am. Like the more he gets to know me, the lamer I'll get.

Charlie tsks. "You can't wear a guitar badge if you don't really play guitar." He raises his right hand and twists his fingers into some kind of weird gang sign. "Scout's honor."

I laugh. "I don't think the Girl Scouts give out badges for my kinds of expertise," I say. And then I get a great idea. "Oh my God, you know what? In the spirit of Halloween, I think subversive badges would be way more appropriate. Like . . . I don't know. Something like a divorced-parents badge."

Charlie recoils in mock horror. "You're not a Girl Scout. You're the anti–Girl Scout." He throws up devil horns. "From hell."

"Exactly," I say, popping up and down on my toes. My good idea is pumping excitement through my whole body. "I could make a therapy badge with someone lying down on a couch!"

"That's awesome. Hey, I could help you if you wanted. We could do them all as buttons."

"That's all right. I've got a mess of felt scraps that Beth gave me to use." Then, there's silence. A pretty uncomfortable one.

It's like I'm programmed to make things as awkward as they can be. "But thanks."

Charlie nods and smiles a little bit. He walks over to another case and pretends to be really interested, even though there are only naked dress forms inside. "Where are you going for Halloween anyway?"

"I'm not sure yet," I lie. I still haven't decided if I should ask Beth if Charlie could come as my date.

"Teddy Baker is having a party, but it'll be stupid. All the Lambert girls are going to show up in plastic slutty nurse outfits and the Fisher guys are dressing up as pimps or Mafia guys." He sighs. "You know, in Pittsburgh my friends and I made a tradition of going to the midnight showing of *Night of the Living Dead* and then we'd all walk the streets as zombies and scare the crap out of people. Every year we had more and more people coming along to haunt the streets with us. It was awesome."

"You miss home?" I ask.

"Yeah. Sometimes. Mostly I miss having my mom around. She was a good buffer between me and my dad. She kept me from having to deal with his tantrums. I guess she needed a break, so I'm kind of handling him in the meantime."

I really want to invite him to Beth's. I mean, I don't think she'll have a problem with it. I like Charlie, and the only reason I'm here with him right now is because of her. This is a good thing. She'll be happy for me.

"Well, I do think my friend Beth is planning on having a party. But you have to come in a costume."

Charlie breaks out into a grin. "Will I be going as your boyfriend? Because if so, I'll need to prepare accordingly."

My face ignites. I try to play off this very awesome and exciting development by examining a Kent brochure on campus recycling procedures. "You can if you want."

"Are you kidding? I'm going to surprise you with the most awesome costume accompaniment in the history of coupledom ever."

We continue to walk the halls, now hand-in-hand. His is a little bit sweaty, but I don't even care. It's like I am living another life with Charlie, one where I don't have any problems or worries. It's an amazing feeling. He leads us to a huge library. We walk inside, past all the kids cramming at big oversized desks or checking their e-mail on rows of computers. We go down into the basement, following the signs for ART SLIDES AND FILMSTRIPS. Charlie walks like he knows exactly where he's going, and leads me into a small viewing room, no bigger than a closet, with only one chair. But we don't need a lot of room. He shuts the door and we kiss for what feels like both forever and a minute.

For the first time, I'm not worried about where my hands should go, or how slobbery I'm getting, or if I'm breathing too heavy out my nose, or if I'll feel ticklish when his hands slide up and down my sides. I let myself be vulnerable.

After a while, we head to the Michener Gallery to see the university's collection of photographs. There's a glass door leading inside. A few other students and some adults mill around the stark white gallery. I've never seen pictures blown up this big before. Each one has its own spotlight and dark black frame.

I'm so glad it's not crowded, because I get to stand in front of each picture and really take it in. Charlie moves a lot faster than me, but I don't mind. I want to take my time. He also offers to hold my book bag — he wears mine on his back and his strapped on his front.

The first really cool photo I see is called *Water and Foam*, by Ansel Adams. I read a little plaque and learn that he's famous for taking landscape pictures. This one is black and white. I can tell it really is what it says — a close-up of running water dotted by swirls of bubbly foam. But it's more than that. It looks other-worldly too, like outer space, complete with shooting stars and the Milky Way. In a very tiny way, it reminds me of the photo I took of that tree that looked like an umbrella. Not saying that I'm anywhere near as amazing as Ansel Adams, of course. But I can understand a little of what he was going for and it makes me feel . . . I don't know . . . smart, I guess.

Another print catches my attention and I make a beeline for it. All you see is a close-up of a girl making a damsel-in-distress sort of face, but the thing you really notice are her eyes. They have very long and very fake eyelashes stuck to them. And she's crying. But instead of real tears, they are drops of silicone or plastic or something. They look completely artificial on purpose.

I love the way this picture makes me feel. Aware of the phoniness of emotions. The photographer's name is Man Ray. I wonder if that's his real name. I definitely want to learn more about him.

Charlie comes over and grabs my hand. "Are you having fun?"

"Oh, yeah!" This is seriously awesome. Looking at all these photographs makes me want to run wild with my own camera. I'm feeling really inspired. I'm so glad we came here, together. Somehow it feels like this never would have happened,

I never would have felt this good today, if not for Charlie. It's totally magical.

We get to the last wall of the gallery. A sign explains that this section features some of the last of Diane Arbus's photographs before she committed suicide. Which is a downer. I guess she had problems too. Maybe all artists do. But I'm really excited to see her work anyway . . . and, like Maria had mentioned, it might be a little bit like mine.

The first print is of four young kids, each wearing homemade Halloween costumes made of paper-bag masks and big sheets. One girl has cut out a couple of bats from black paper and stuck them on her dress. It's pretty cute. The next is of a single overweight girl, wrapped up in a sheet and wearing a mask, standing in a field. It's weird and sad.

When I step over to the next print, my smile fades.

I notice now that the people featured in these particular pictures are mentally retarded. There's a shot of them smiling and running through a field with their masks, innocent and happy, like little kids would be. But they are older. Some probably older than me. And their faces are soft in a way that tells you something's wrong with them.

I let go of Charlie's hand and step over to the next print. Now the people look less happy. They look like they don't know what's going on. One young guy has an old-fashioned mustache drawn sloppily across his mouth. An older woman in a black mask is leading him forward, and he's just kind of dragging limply behind her.

"This isn't right," I say and turn to Charlie.

"I know, it's insane, right?"

"No. It's. Not. Right."

"Wait . . ." Charlie says slowly and carefully, sensing how upset I am. "Talk to me. What's not right?"

"I mean, everyone's happy and smiling and having a good time, but you know." I turn away from him and stare deep into the photograph.

"Ruby, don't feel bad for them. Look, they're having fun."

I shrug off his shoulder and try to walk through the gallery, but my eyes well up and pour out big fat tears. I am such an idiot.

Charlie puts his hand on my shoulder again but doesn't let me shrug it off this time. Instead, he pushes me and tries to look me in the face. I drop my chin and try to bury myself in the collar of my jacket.

"What's wrong?"

"She's just using these poor people. She's exploiting them because she thinks they don't know better."

"Well, yeah. A lot of her pictures are like that. But she doesn't only take pictures of retarded people, Ruby. She did portraits of cross-dressers, midgets, and nudists — all kinds of crazy people. It's like she was obsessed with weirdness."

"But don't you see? She's not just showing us them, and the weird things or sad things about them. She's forcing us to view things in a certain way. Her way." I rub some of the tears out of my eyes. These pictures are making me feel terrible. I have to get out of here before I completely lose it. When I open them, Charlie takes a big open picture of my red wet face with my camera.

"What are you doing?" I shout, throwing my hands up and nearly knocking my camera out of his hands. The other people in the gallery turn and stare at us.

"I know it sounds crazy, but hurt and pain can be good things. They put us in touch with ourselves. Why do you think my dad is able to express himself so well though printing? Because he's miserable."

"I don't want to be miserable! And I don't want people manipulating me to feel a certain way!"

"No, of course not. But being able to look at something and have feelings is like a basic component of art." He shakes his head. "Listen. I know you're scared of feeling something, something you're afraid everyone can see, but you can't let that fear hold you back. It's part of who you are."

He shows me the picture of myself. And to my surprise, I don't look like a complete mess. I look, well, alive. A hot rush of everything hits me at once. All the pictures and memories have been pulling me to this moment of actually looking at what's happened. I'm not wearing a goofy face like a mask, or staging the perfect smile for someone else. I'm just being me.

Charlie leads me out of the gallery and over to the big lawn. I feel it's about a million degrees, so I peel off my peacoat and scarf and leave them in a pile on the grass. He sits me down and waits for me to talk.

It doesn't take long.

I open up and tell him everything. I tell him about Jim, about him leaving and how badly it messed me up. I tell him about all the other memories that have been holding me hostage. I tell him Jim's staying in a hotel across town and that I'm not supposed to know it. I tell him that Beth has my letter. That she stole it. And I don't know what to do.

Talking to Charlie is nothing like talking to Beth. He doesn't nod or even shake his head. Best of all, he doesn't interrupt with his take on things, or try to force me to see things from his point of view. He just listens. It's amazing. And my mind, which usually shuts down or does what it's told, spirals all over the place in a frenzy that is madness and liberation and relief.

For the first time, I admit out loud that maybe Beth doesn't really know what's good for me anymore. Once it's out there, in the air, I know it's true. It sounds true. It feels true. And while it's totally sad, it also gives me courage to face what that really means.

I need to tell Beth that I know she has my letter.

TWENTY-FOUR

While Mr. Eid takes attendance from behind his wooden podium and the rest of the kids in my homeroom joke around or finish their homework, I rip out a sheet of notebook paper and gnaw the cap of my pen.

After a ridiculous amount of deliberation, I scribble:

Beth — Meet me in the library @ lunch — URGENT!

I fold the note into a tight triangle and put it in the front pocket of my hooded sweatshirt. Then I pull my book bag up on my lap and hug it tight. The pointy corners of my cardboard box poke through the nylon. As the clock on the wall ticks home-room down the final minute, I second-guess myself and what I'm about to do.

The thing is, I decided that I didn't want to call Beth out showdown style. I just want her to come clean about having the letter of her own accord, and if I have to lead her into admitting the truth, I'm okay with that.

Beth had left me a couple of messages last night to make sure I was feeling better and she dropped off my assignments to my mom when I went to bed early. It was really nice of her to go through all the trouble. I so wanted to trust her again. I hated having those kinds of feelings, and I knew they were ruining what was left of our friendship. Now that I was letting myself deal with the truth, the truth was that I still cared about what was left. I cared about her.

So I came up with a plan. I'd show Beth the box Jim left for me and play dumb. I'd pretend I didn't know anything about his letter, and when I asked her what she thought about everything, she'd have to tell me about it, or at the very least give me a clue why she stole it in the first place.

Homeroom bell rings, and it's time to head to first period. I go in the opposite direction of History, toward the English wing, where Beth's classroom is, and plant myself in the doorway.

"Hi!" Beth says as she approaches. "What's up? Couldn't get enough of me on the ride to school?"

"For you." I hand her the note and she smiles. Beth loves notes. I smile back, even though it feels like lying.

I'm walking back toward my classroom when a pair of hands covers my eyes from behind. I can tell who it is by the smell of gingerbread.

"Maria?"

"Ha!" she says, spinning me around. "So, you feeling any better? What'd you have — mono? Catch the make-out disease from your new boy?"

I fake cough for her. "Hardly. Just the flu."

"Well, how are things going with Charlie?"

"Fine, I guess." I watch Maria's smile fade as I don't give her any more details. I know she'd LOVE to hear the story of my

Kent afternoon, about my crazy reaction to Diane Arbus, but I can't say anything. It's a wonder she still likes me. Our friendship is totally one-sided. "Well, I did invite Charlie to the party. Like you said."

"And did he say yes?"

I nod and smile. Maria nearly knocks me over with a huge hug.

"Only thing is . . . I haven't asked Beth yet if he can come."

"She's not going to care. She'll be happy for you."

"I don't know. Remember how weird she got during the car ride when you first mentioned it?"

She puckers her lips. "Whatever. I think I'm going to invite Davey, even though she thinks I'm wasting my time on him. You know, we still haven't kissed? I don't know what's wrong with him. Maybe he really does just want to be friends."

"He's probably nervous. Because you're, you know . . . so *experienced.*" I bite on my fingernail. "Wait. That came out wrong."

Maria just laughs. "No, I get it. Maybe that's it. I doubt Davey's kissed many girls. He's kind of quiet and shy, like you." She shakes her head. "Anyhow, I don't think you have anything to worry about with Beth. But tell her in front of me, if you want. I'll act so excited that she definitely won't say anything negative."

I could hug her. I do hug her. "Thanks, Maria."

A thought flashes across my brain like lightning. I pull back a chunk of thick black hair from her ear and lean in. "Hey," I whisper. "Do me a favor, okay, and meet me in the library during lunch. There's something I want to talk to you about." I let her hair fall back and spot a tall blond girl strutting down the hallway toward us, looking pissed as usual. "And don't tell Katherine."

Maria looks pretty surprised, but also encouraging. She gives my arm a squeeze. "That's so funny! I was just going to ask you what we were doing for Beth's birthday. 'Cause since it falls on a Saturday, we'll have to decorate her locker and all that stuff tomorrow."

"Oh," I say, having totally spaced. "Right." I'm so glad Maria reminded me. If I messed that up, Beth would never let me live it down. She takes that kind of stuff really seriously. Thank God I still have an extra day to prepare.

"Wait. You wanted to talk to me about something else?" Now Maria looks really interested.

"Umm, yeah, kind of."

Maria notices me watching Katherine get closer and closer. She gives me a discreet little wink. "Okay! See you in the library."

I walk away feeling nervous, but also glad I invited her along. Maria's reaction to the box full of junk might work in my favor. Beth wouldn't be able to get as pushy as she does sometimes when we're alone. And it will be nice to finally show Maria that I really do consider her a friend too.

Once the lunch bell rings, I pack up my books and head to the library. It's not that crowded, only a table or two of over-zealous freshmen who already wear sweatshirts from their Ivy Leagues of choice. I make my way inconspicuously to the back stacks, near the 1970s encyclopedia sets that no one uses anymore.

I sit down on the carpet with my book bag in my lap and wait for them to arrive.

Beth is first. She plops down next to me and gives me a big, tender hug. I smile at her and look down at my lap, trying to rally my courage. She pins back the front pieces of her hair and gives me a few seconds to start talking on my own. When I don't say anything, she looks a little bit annoyed.

"Soooo," she draws out, "you've got me totally freaking worried all morning. I couldn't even concentrate on my bio quiz. And now you're going to make me pull it out of you?"

"Wait a second and I'll explain everything."

Beth's top lip curls up, exposing her fleshy pink gums. "Wait? For what?"

If this were the old days, Beth would be the only one I needed. I know she's not going to like having to share the stage with someone else. Just then, Maria rounds the corner. Beth looks surprised to see her, but quickly wipes the look off her face.

"Hey," Maria says, sliding down on the floor next to me. She's got a skirt on but she doesn't even try to close her legs. I guess it's because she's wearing tights.

"Okay," I say, my voice quivering. I unzip my bag and pull out the cardboard box. I'm instantly as upset as I was when I first looked inside it. "I found this on my front stoop yesterday."

"What's that?" Beth asks. Her voice isn't curious. It's defensive.

"It's from Jim," I say, trying not to look directly at Beth.

"Really?" Maria asks, biting her lip. She puts her hand near the box slowly, as if it were hot. "Can I —"

"Yeah," I say. "Go ahead."

I lean back on my hands while Beth and Maria tilt forward, poring over the contents of the box.

"Why didn't you call me back last night and tell me this had happened?" Beth asks. She raises two fists full of stuff and then lets it fall.

I shrug. "I didn't know what to make of it all."

"Maybe this box wasn't even meant for you," Beth says. "Maybe this was for your mom." It's a ridiculous thing to say and she knows it. Before I can answer her, Maria pushes the flap of the box down and points to the place where Jim carved RUBY in blue pen. "Oh." She says it kind of annoyed.

"Did he leave a note or anything?" Maria asks me.

"Nope." I glance at Beth out of the corner of my eye, but she just adjusts her position on the carpet and stays quiet.

Maria looks to me and Beth, silently asking for permission to give her opinion. She's being so respectful and careful about everything. I nod and tell her to go ahead.

"Well, I think it's safe to say that your dad . . . Jim . . . whatever you want to say, must still be in Akron somewhere. And he seems pretty intent on talking to you. So I guess we should figure out where he is and take you there, and you either sit down and hear what he has to say, or tell him off for good."

This is exactly the discussion I want to have. But before I can say anything, Beth puts her hand on my knee and shakes her head dismissively at Maria. "If he really wanted to see her, he would have told her where to find him. Sorry, but I think this is just a passive-aggressive way to mess with her head." She stretches her arms. "Like I've been saying all along, you should just forget him."

My mouth drops open as Beth holds up the silver watch to her ear and listens for a nonexistent ticking. I can't believe she's still lying! "But what if he has something important to tell me?" I ask.

She actually laughs. "What? Like why he left? Why he never bothered to call?" Beth rolls her eyes. "What kind of enlightening tidbit do you think you're going to get, Ruby? And more important, is knowing that really going to help you?"

"It'll be closure."

"Closure? I thought you *had* closure. It all seems like a pretty done deal to me."

I look at Maria. She's just thumbing through the box stuff over and over. I know she's afraid to get into this. She might even regret that I asked her here in the first place.

"Well, I was talking to Charlie . . ."

"What?" Beth asks quietly. "So you told Charlie about the box right away, but you didn't think to call me?" She rolls her eyes. "Honestly, Ruby. I don't really care what your boyfriend of approximately two days has told you to do. I'm the only one here who has been by your side this whole time, helping you put your life back together." She tosses items lying around on the carpet back inside the box. "Listen, maybe this makes me sound like a jerk, but I'm kind of tired of saying the same stuff to you over and over again. You're either going to listen to me or do what you want. And that's fine, but I'm not going to waste my energy anymore trying to help you if you're just going to ignore what I say."

"I don't get it," I say, because I honestly can't believe what I'm hearing. This is worse than any lie she could have told me. "Are you giving me an ultimatum?"

Maria clears her throat. "I think what Beth's trying to say is that she just doesn't want you to get hurt again. None of us do, Ruby."

"What's this? Some kind of powwow?" I glance up and Katherine is standing right in front of us. She looks pissed. "Who called this little meeting?" Maria's eyes fall to her lap, but Beth stares right in my direction. "Thanks for inviting me, Ruby!"

I can't shove the box into my book bag quick enough.

Katherine leans against a bookshelf and sneers. "I've been looking all over for you guys. But, seriously, Ruby. What's with the diss? I'm not cool enough for your little show-and-tell?"

I stand up first. Katherine tries to block my way, her body filling the open space between two stacks of books, but I just duck under her arm and keep walking, like she doesn't even exist.

TWENTY-FIVE

After the last-period bell, I take my time walking to my locker. The hallway feels too crowded, with people yelling and screaming louder than I've ever heard them before. I stick my fingers in my ears and walk close to the wall, keeping my head down until I reach my locker. After twirling my combination, I sink to the floor and pull textbooks from the bottom where they've been chucked.

I think about just walking home alone, but when I stand up and slam the door closed, Beth's waiting behind it, leaning against the locker next to mine. I don't know who goes first but we both turn and walk to the front door together. We don't talk.

It's like Beth has turned into my mom or something.

Today is probably the coldest day of the year. Maria is already inside her car, I guess to keep warm. I fold up the collar of my peacoat up around my neck and then stop dead in my tracks.

Beth's scarf. It's missing. I must have left it on the lawn at Kent State.

I feel terrible, probably more than I should, but there's nothing much I can do now. Maybe Charlie picked it up and forgot to give it back to me. I hope I can find it before she notices.

Katherine's in shotgun, laughing into her cell phone and holding her hands up to the heating vents. She should be in the Period Seat, but I guess she's trying to make a statement or something. So I slide in and take her spot, making sure I keep my neck hidden by my long hair.

Katherine clicks her cell phone closed and spins around to stare at me. "Hey, Maria and Beth, you want to go hang out at my house?" No one says anything, but Katherine cackles. "Seriously, I can't wait to tell you this secret, just as soon as we drop Ruby off."

I grind my teeth. I know I'm not going to say anything to Katherine, but I really want to smack her in the face.

"Shut up, Katherine," Beth says in a quiet, tired voice.

"What? I'm just saying — "

"Well, don't. Don't say anything."

Maria heads to my house first. A mercy drop-off, thank God. Charlie is there, sitting on the grass in his cute uniform, with his BMX tossed casually to the side. He flips through some papers on his lap, and he keeps brushing his floppy hair out of his eyes. My heart races a little bit. One nice surprise.

"Thanks for the ride," I say, exiting the car and slinging my book bag over my shoulder.

Beth glances at Charlie and then she turns away from me. "So I guess you're not coming over?"

I duck back into the doorway. "Was I supposed to come over today?" I don't think we had plans. In fact, I'm sure of it. She defended me a moment ago, and now she's trying to start a fight? I don't get it.

Beth doesn't say anything. Not even good-bye. So I just close the door.

The girls pull away and Charlie waves. I plod toward him, trudging every step like my New Balances are filled with cement.

He sticks his arm out and pulls me down onto the crispy grass. "Rough day?"

I let myself fall into him. "I guess."

"Did you say anything to Beth?"

"Yes, but I don't want to talk about that."

He nods his head and hands me the stack of papers. "I Googled your dad last night. Didn't come up with much, but I found a few articles where he's mentioned in the forestry service and stuff. I think he was once stationed at Crater Lake National Park."

He hands me the papers, but I don't take them. "So?"

"So . . . I thought you might want to read up before you saw him."

I cross my arms. "Who said I was going to go see him? I never said that."

"I know that, Ruby. I'm just saying if you decide to."

"Hey! You didn't happen to pick up my scarf from off the ground when we were at Kent, did you?"

"No . . . why? Did you lose it?"

My heart sinks. "Let's just go inside," I say, pulling him by the arm.

"Are you sure? I can leave you alone if you want. You seem like you've got a lot on your mind."

My mind is overflowing, but I don't want to be alone. Because then I'd have to think about stuff. "Nonononono. Please. Come in."

"Good," he says and folds up the papers and tucks them into his coat pocket.

I use the spare key and Charlie stands quietly behind me. Once we are inside the house, it doesn't take us very long before we are making out. Just enough for him to take off his coat, get the quick tour of the downstairs, and for me to ask him if he wants something to drink.

But kissing Charlie against the cupboards doesn't feel as good as it did when we were at Kent State. I guess all my problems are way too close to me now. So I press my mouth against his harder and harder and push down on his shoulders until we are both on the kitchen floor. My hands are going crazy, rubbing all over his back and arms.

The automatic door clicks open from the garage underneath the house. The vibrations scatter over the kitchen floor and up through my skin. I should stop kissing him, but I don't.

"I think your mom's home." Charlie pulls back away from my face but I push on him until he rolls onto his back. "Hey!" he says, plucking my fingers off his shiny, metallic Western belt buckle. "What are you doing?"

I laugh, but it doesn't sound like my voice. And I hold on tighter.

Footsteps creak up the stairs, but I want to push the envelope. The door opens. Charlie tries to pull away but I won't let him. My short brittle fingernails dig into his neck.

A gasp escapes from my mom at the sight of us in a tangle on the floor. "Ruby!" Her face is twisted up and she covers her eyes with her hand, like we're naked or something.

Charlie breaks free and stands up. "Hello," he says, his voice shaking. And then "I should go" quickly thereafter. "I'll call you later, Ruby."

This time I let him. Mom is staring at me. Her eyes are welling up. When the front door opens and closes, she says, "You know that boys are not allowed in this house when I'm not here."

"Sorry, I forgot you were running a convent."

"Ruby —"

She ruined her life, but I'm not going to let her ruin mine. "Mom, just because you're afraid to be with guys doesn't mean I am too."

"Don't talk to me like that."

"Fine. I won't talk at all. I know you like it better that way." I stand up, snatch Charlie's papers, and go to my room to finish my costume.

TWENTY-SIX

We're parked outside of Katherine's house and she's taking forever.

I shield the morning sun from my tired eyes and discreetly flip through the stack of pictures hidden in the front pocket of my book bag. I almost forgot the locker-decorating stuff again this morning, but thankfully Maria called to remind me. So on my way out of the house, I grabbed a bunch of random old pictures of me and Beth, along with some streamers and curly ribbons and a roll of tape. Though the whole sentiment feels totally phony.

I should have decorated yesterday, so Beth would arrive and be surprised this morning. But her birthday was about the last thing on my mind. I'm actually not thinking too much about it now, either. I'm just flipping through picture after picture of what our friendship used to be like. Even ones we took last May, during our freshman trip to Lake Erie, seem old and nostalgic.

"Should I call Katherine or something?" Maria asks, tapping her horn again. "I really can't be late today." She catches my attention in her rearview mirror and rolls her eyes. Maria was supposed to stop by the office this morning and fill out a slip so that the PA announcers would mention Beth's birthday over the loudspeakers during homeroom. But at this rate, it's not going to happen. We're not even going to make homeroom.

"Here she comes," Beth says, pointing across Maria's lap.

Katherine's front door flings open wide and bangs against the outside railing. Her arms are flailing wildly, and she's pointing and screaming at someone inside I can't see. A little girl with white-blonde hair up in a sloppy, slept-on ponytail runs past the front door in a lilac nightgown and ballet slippers. She's hysterical and grabs onto Katherine's legs. But Katherine doesn't seem to notice, too focused on whatever argument she's in the middle of. She eventually shakes her sister free, steps outside, and pulls the front door closed so hard that the brass door knocker taps down three times. Then she stalks down the driveway, squeezing her book bag to her chest. As she passes in between the two cars parked side-by-side in her driveway, she kicks the old chocolate-brown sedan in the passenger-side door as hard as she can.

"Uh-oh," Maria says quietly, unlocking the back door. I slide over to the Period Seat, even though it's Katherine's second turn in a row skipping it.

Katherine gets inside and fumbles for a cigarette, her hands raw and red and chapped. She pushes down the lighter on the console in between us and chews on the end of her filter while she waits for it to heat up.

"Are you all right?" Beth asks, turning around from the front seat. She tries to brush away a piece of Katherine's hair from her eyes.

Katherine leans back, just out of Beth's reach. The lighter pops up. She ignites her cigarette and takes a huge drag that leaves behind a long line of gray ash. "I'm fine," she says calmly, smoke pouring out the sides of her mouth. "Here," she adds, fishing something purple and sparkly out of her pocket. She hands it to Beth.

"What's this?"

"Just a bow I got at the drugstore last night. I thought you could pin it to your shirt or something today. For your fake school birthday."

"Thank you so much!" Beth says, flipping down the visor and pinning the bow on her red polka-dotted blouse. I hug my book bag and watch the clock on the dashboard. I'll have to figure out a way to decorate her locker before Beth notices. I can't let Katherine show me up.

"You're welcome. Now, listen. I have a favor to ask. About tonight."

With one more day until the party, the plan is to spend the night at Beth's house so we can take care of any last-minute pre-party stuff like the food, our costumes, and a good mix for the dance floor. We are also going to dip into the little airplane bottles and laugh our way though the lame and unscary Halloween movie marathon that always runs on cable.

"Okay," Maria says, stopping at a yellow light. "What's up?"

"Well, do you guys usually go out and mess around on Mischief Night?"

Beth takes a spiral curl and coils it around her finger. "I think last year we TPed someone's house."

Maria laughs and changes the radio station. "It was Joey's house. And he totally deserved it, remember?"

I don't really remember who Joey is. And honestly I don't know how Maria does it. I couldn't imagine kissing anyone other than Charlie. Could she possibly like all the guys she dates? Is Davey really someone special to her, or are they all just interchangeable warm bodies?

Beth turns to face Katherine. "Why?"

Katherine cracks the window, sending a rush of cold air pouring into our toasty car. "Because I've got a prank I want to pull on my dad, but I'm going to need your help."

"Oh, Katherine, I don't know . . ." Beth says.

"I'm not going to do anything crazy, okay? I'm just going to cover his stupid-ass car in shaving cream so he won't be able to sleep over at my mom's tonight."

"Don't you think he'll just clean up the shaving cream and drive over anyway, if he really wants to see her?" I ask.

Katherine completely ignores me. "They spent all last night fighting and screaming at each other, because my mom wants him to move back in, but he says he wants his independence and whatever. I could barely sleep, and of course my sister and brother are freaking out. Then this morning, they're making plans for a 'date night' tonight like nothing happened. It drives me crazy!"

"But, what about — "

"And we'll still be able to finish all the stuff for the party and everything. Don't worry, Beth. It will seriously take like five minutes out of our night."

"Umm," Beth says, drumming her fingers on the window. "I still don't know . . ."

"Come on! This'll be fun!"

"I don't think this is a good idea." I say this really loud, so I can't be ignored anymore. I can just see Katherine freaking out and things getting scary.

"I honestly don't care what you think, Ruby."

"Well, I'm not going."

"Who says you're invited, anyway?"

"Fine with me," I mumble. "Whatever."

Nobody says anything else for the rest of the ride. I'm all kinds of uncomfortable, sitting there next to Katherine. She's obviously trying to make me feel excluded because of how things went down yesterday at the library. I hate that it's working.

Just as we walk in the doors to school, homeroom bell rings.

"Hey, we should all probably go right to class," I say, hoisting my book bag onto my shoulders. Thanks to Katherine, we're officially late, and I don't want Beth to go to her locker. Maybe I'll have a chance to decorate it before her next class, if I can convince Mr. Reynolds to give me a bathroom pass. He's such a Nazi, it's like he doesn't believe in peeing.

"I need a pencil," she says.

"I've got one you can borrow in my book bag!" I call out, but she's already running down the hall. She doesn't need a pencil. She wants to see how I've returned the favor for all the awesome birthday stuff she did for me last week. My stomach rolls over.

Of course, her locker looks like everyone else's — plain gray institutional metal. She stares at it like she's waiting for something to happen, for some birthday surprise to materialize.

"Beth, if it wasn't for Katherine being late, I could have — "

"No." She shakes me off. "It's cool. You could have done it yesterday, but you wanted to hang out with your boyfriend or whatever."

I try to stammer out an apology. I actually feel really bad about this, regardless of all the crap going on between us. Not decorating your best friend's locker on her birthday is a huge jerky thing to do.

She plants her hands on her hips. "And don't think I haven't noticed that you've stopped wearing your scarf. What's wrong? Did you lose it?"

I shake my head, but I know she doesn't believe me. She just gets angrier and walks away from me, toward her class. "Whatever, Ruby. I guess I'll just call you later or something." The way she says it, all sharp and pointy, makes me know that I'm not going to get a call. I'm going to get the *or something*.

TWENTY-SEVEN

I call Charlie as soon as I get home from school because I'm upset and I definitely don't want to sit in my house alone. He answers the phone really quick, like he's in the middle of something. But he tells me to come right over, which is exactly what I want to do.

I dump my school books onto my bed and pack up my sleepover stuff, my costume, and my camera into my book bag, just in case I end up at Beth's later when they're done pranking Katherine's dad. But I doubt I will. Beth is obviously pissed at me for the birthday stuff and the lost scarf. And while Maria was cool about everything that went down in the library, she doesn't seem to get what a big deal this all is to me. It's like if it isn't boy drama, it doesn't register as being important in her brain. And I seriously can't even handle Katherine and all her family issues because I've got more than enough of my own to worry about.

A big part of me just wants to stay over at Charlie's house tonight and just forget about everyone else. I bet his dad would let me, too. He's pretty unconventional, like the kind of parent who wouldn't think boy-girl sleepovers are weird and inappropriate. I'd just have to say really nice things about his art. Or maybe he'd be working in his studio all night and have no clue I was even there. I'd stay up in Charlie's bedroom and we'd make buttons and listen to music and he'd have to sneak downstairs and steal us snacks from the kitchen. And then we'd snuggle in the same bed together, spooning and kissing and fooling around all night long in between power naps. It'd be awesome.

Charlie lives across town, so riding my bike will be the quickest way to get there. My bike should be on the side of the house, where I last left it, but it's missing. I check the garage and find it buried behind a waist-high pile of miscellaneous crap. Mom must have put it away for me.

A roar in the distance grows louder. I turn to face it and a bright flash burns my eyes. The headlights of a car bounce over the curb and up our bumpy driveway, but I'm too blinded to make out who it is. The car slowly rolls to a stop halfway up the gravel and the headlights flick off. I squint away the spots.

My mom comes into focus, dressed in jeans, a red cardigan, and her favorite brown boots. Her hair is in a loose ponytail at the nape of her neck, though most of the shorter pieces that frame her face have fallen out and flutter in the wind. She's carrying two overstuffed grocery bags in her arms.

"Ruby, it's too late for you to be riding your bike in those dark clothes." She positions herself behind me and watches as I kick aside scraps of wood, a rake, and some dirty rags. Once I've chipped away most of the junk, I give a sharp tug on the handlebars, but the bike doesn't move. A warped garden hose has snaked itself inside the spokes of the front wheel. "Honey. Just let me drive you over to Beth's."

"I'm not going to Beth's," I say. I kick an empty watering can and it sails into one of the windows, bouncing off instead of breaking it. Still, it's pretty dramatic. "And what is all this crap you've buried my bike with? I mean, really. I don't think I've ever seen you use this thing," I say, jabbing my finger at a partially inflated exercise ball.

Mom sets the groceries down on the concrete and crouches to help me liberate my bike from the tether. I step back and let her work, my arms folded across my chest, annoyed as hell.

"Where are you going then? I don't want you messing around on Mischief Night, getting yourself into trouble."

"I'm going to my boyfriend's house," I say.

"Ruby, I've only met this boy once, and he didn't necessarily make the best impression on me. Anyhow, I thought you were sleeping over at Beth's house. Is everything okay between you two?"

Why is she so suspicious of Charlie? He's definitely the best thing that's happened to me in a long time. A big dark cloud rumbles up from my chest into my mouth. "Everything's fine, Mom. Charlie found some info about Jim for me on the Internet. I think that's more important than a stupid sleepover, don't you?"

Mom doesn't react, which is not at all surprising. Her focus is on untangling the hose from the spokes of my wheel. It's proving more difficult than she thought. She pulls and tugs on the hose as hard as she can, and her face reddens with the effort.

"Charlie wants to go with me to see him. Over break. His parents already said yes." Okay, that's not at all true. But I bet Charlie would come with me to see Jim, if I asked him to. He's that kind of guy.

Mom rocks backward and gives one last pull, as hard as she can. The slack in the hose goes taut and I watch as a kink works itself free from the spokes. Mom suddenly flies backward and falls on her butt with a thud. She stands up, her face all scrunched with pain, and dusts off her jeans. "Be home by ten, then."

I might as well be talking to a brick wall. "All of a sudden you don't care where I'm going?"

"You think just because you're sixteen that you don't have a curfew?"

"No, I think you'd rather talk about anything but Dad!"

She walks back over to the car and starts it. The headlights come back on and she waits patiently for me to ride out of the beams with my bike so she can park in the space I'm occupying. Her windows are rolled up tight.

This conversation is over. I pedal away as fast as I can.

Even if Charlie hadn't told me what house number was his, I certainly could have guessed. His house is big and modern, with lots of tinted glass windows and exposed metal beams. It's really beautiful and dramatic, but not very homey.

Charlie is waiting for me on the steps when I get there. He's got a sheet over his head with two eye holes cut out. I wonder if this is his costume for tomorrow's party. It doesn't really go with my Girl Scout outfit, but it's still really cute.

I set my bike down in the grass and fish my camera out from my bag. This is going to make the best picture. Totally frameable or locker-worthy. I walk up his steps, center him in a shot, and pull the trigger.

"Hi," I say, and fan the picture.

He pulls the sheet over his head. "Boo," he says in a soft, sad voice. And then he looks down at his sneakers. I run up to his side and give him a hug. "What's wrong? Are you okay?"

"Come on," he says, sniffing and smiling at the same time. "Let's go inside. I've got something to tell you."

"All right," I say, even though I don't want to. Even though I feel like I'm walking right into a trap.

The house looks just like two messy artistic boys live here alone. The place is covered in stuff, moving boxes unopened in big stacks against the wall. Take-out containers are everywhere and it smells like incense.

Charlie's dad has some weird French record blasting on the stereo, and he's drinking a huge glass of red wine. He does an awkward little shuffle around the dining room table, where one of his huge landscapes is spread out, as if his stiff body isn't used to acting happy. He rolls the print up carefully and slides it into a cardboard tube. Like the one I put my map in when we moved.

I follow Charlie up the wooden stairs, passing by shelves full of twisted and gnarled metal sculptures that I guess are his mom's work. His room is the messiest yet. I thought Charlie only made buttons, but there are paintings and prints and pieces of ripped-up fabric everywhere. He kicks the stuff aside, crashes down on his bed, and cradles his head in his hands.

He pats the bed next to him. But I don't want to sit down. "What is it?"

"My dad's been rehired at Carnegie-Mellon. They called him today to offer him that promotion he wanted. Turns out that the guy they hired over him was a total hack."

"Oh, yeah?" I say almost too casually as I take off my peacoat. I lock my eyes on a weird, home-sewn stuffed animal atop

Charlie's pillow. He's making a cute face right in my direction. I throw my coat over it.

Charlie raises his head and stares at me all weird, like I should be crying or something. "Yeah. Yeah, Ruby. We're going to be moving back at the end of this semester."

"So you're breaking up with me?" There's a part of me that can't believe it. And then there's a part of me that knew this was coming all along.

He shakes his head emphatically. "I didn't say that."

"Well, how are we going to date when you live in another state, Charlie? I don't have a car and that's kinda far for your BMX."

His head falls into his hands. "I don't know, okay? But we'll figure something out."

My throat nearly closes up with the size of the lump that settles there. This is exactly the kind of thing Beth had tried to warn me about. "I guess I'm going to go," I say, and reach for my peacoat. I was stupid to take it off in the first place.

"Wait! Why?"

"Because, Charlie. I'm not going to keep on liking you or whatever if you're just going to turn around and move somewhere else. That would be pretty stupid."

"Ruby, I don't get you. I said I'm not leaving for a few months. And you're just going to end things now? I thought you really liked me."

I don't say anything to that, and Charlie gets mad. He grumbles under his breath and kicks the art supplies that are in reach of his feet.

But I'm already moving down the stairs, out the front door. I pick up my bike and ride to the only place I have left to go.

TWENTY-EIGHT

I get to Beth's house and park my bike in her driveway. I don't know why, but instead of just walking in the back door like I usually do, I go around to the front of the house and ring the bell like I'm a stranger. It's probably because I'm not sure if I'm even welcome here.

Mrs. Miller and Martha race to the foyer. They were watching television in the main room. I can hear the laugh track from outside. The door opens and the two of them greet me with wry smiles.

"Is Beth upstairs?"

"Ruby! We were wondering where you were!"

"Is she upstairs?" I say again, this time in a whisper.

Mrs. Miller wrinkles up her face. "Yes, dear, of course. Go right on up." Then she winks to lighten the formality. "Third door on the left, you know."

I walk up the staircase slowly, stopping to look at all the family portraits hanging on the walls. The Millers are incredibly photogenic. And happy. I'm included in lots of the shots, when they let me tag along on a family trip or ski weekend. It's obvious I don't really belong, because I've been taller than everyone in Beth's family since junior high, including her dad, but I look just as happy as they do. It makes my heart hurt.

The girls are whispering inside Beth's room. I press my ear to the closed door, but I can't make out anything but mumbles. Martha's coming up the stairs after me, so I have to knock. There's rustling and some suspicious sounds. Then I open the door. "Hi," I say, stepping into the room and closing the door behind me.

Everyone's surprised to see me. The girls are all dressed in black. Katherine's gym bag is open on the bed, filled with cans of shaving cream.

"Hey, Ruby," Maria says, nice and friendly. "You made it!"

"I thought you weren't coming," Beth groans.

"Yeah, well." I take off my peacoat and toss my bag in the corner. "I changed my mind. Is that okay with you?"

"I said you could do whatever you want, remember?"

Katherine rubs a little moisturizer underneath her eyes. "Geez. What's up with you two? I'm the one who's supposed to be mad here." She laughs, and I can tell she's over the whole library incident. Or maybe she's just more entertained by the fact that there's something going on between me and Beth.

"Nothing's up," Beth says. "I'm just surprised. I didn't think Ruby was planning to celebrate my birthday this year." She walks over to her dresser and starts straightening piles of stuff that already look pretty neat to me. "You know how excited I was for this weekend. And it's like you couldn't care less about me now that you have a boyfriend."

"I broke up with him," I say. "Tonight." I look down at my feet and get choked up, but I squeeze all the muscles in my face to try and hold it together.

"Oh." Beth thinks for a second, then hands me a box of tissues.

Maria gasps. "What happened?"

"It doesn't even matter," I say through big wet sniffles.

"That sucks," Katherine says softly.

Beth takes a deep, contemplative breath, the kind that always precede her lectures. I close my eyes and brace myself. But all she says, in the most quiet whisper, is "I'm sorry."

Her words practically knock me over. Whether or not they mean what I hope they mean, they are what I need right now. I look into her eyes and apologize too.

Beth's face goes soft. "Don't worry about it," she says, throwing her arms around me. "Seriously, not at all. I'm just glad you're here and that everything's cool between us. You know I hate when we fight!"

"Me too," I say, and squeeze her back.

"Do you want to change into one of my black sweaters? You know, for stealth's sake?"

"Yeah, okay. Thanks." I duck into her huge closet and go through all the sweaters folded on the shelves. There's one fuzzy black angora cardigan that I love. It's like wearing your favorite stuffed animal. When I pull that out from the stack, a few sweaters fall. I stoop over to pick them up and find myself eye-level with a shoe box on one of the lower shelves.

A really cute picture of me and Beth is pasted to the top of the box. We've both got bright red cheeks and we're nestled together inside an igloo. I'm about to inspect it further when the door flings open.

"Let's go! The original *Nightmare on Elm Street* with Johnny Depp starts at eight and I don't want to miss it!" Beth gives me a weird look, seeing me on the floor.

I grab all the fallen sweaters in my hand and jump to my feet. "These fell."

"No problem," she says, taking them out of my hands and stuffing them back into place.

We sneak down the back staircase and hop into the Volvo. I volunteer to take the Period Seat as a testament to general goodwill. Katherine twirls the radio dial and stops on a band I don't know, but the music has a crazy thumping bass guitar and I'm actually getting excited. Or at least I'm looking forward to a little mischief at someone else's expense.

Katherine sits in shotgun and gives Maria directions to the gross apartment bungalows near the swampy lake. A few people have already been out pranking, because long dangles of TP flutter in the sky and a few cracked pumpkins splatter the street.

Katherine points out the windshield and Maria slows. Her father's brown car is parked under a tree. We pull up a few feet away from it and kill the headlights.

The street is pretty quiet, except for a few people walking to the corner store up the street and two kids having an egg fight on a driveway.

"Okay. This is it!" Katherine squeals.

Beth passes out a can of shaving cream to each of us.

"Make sure you get all the windows and door handles. I want this thing to be totally undriveable." Katherine shakes up her can and pulls her sweatshirt hood over her long blond hair. I've never seen her look so genuinely happy and excited. "Ready?"

We all nod.

Katherine shouts "Ready! Set!" but by "Go!" she's already out of the car, leaving us to catch up. I take the driver's-side door and smear a huge dollop of cream across it. Beth is on the back windshield, painting it with long back and forth strokes. Maria is on the opposite side of me, doing the same to the passenger side. Katherine drags her fingers through the cream, branding the front windshield with a bunch of curses.

Before I know it, I'm laughing, 'cause in a weird way, this actually feels like a release. Katherine's dad *is* a jerk. He totally deserves this. I start to get really into it, pressing the nozzle down as hard as I can. I try to draw a hand giving the middle finger, but it looks stupid so I just make a bunch of big goofy loops with the foam.

After a minute or two, my can sputters empty. I haven't covered as much of the car as I wanted, so I sweep my hand and spread out the cream until every inch of my panel is covered, at least a little bit.

"I'm all out!" Beth whispers.

"Me too," says Maria.

I wipe my hands on some big leaves from the pile at my feet and then pull out my camera from my book bag and take a few shots. The car looks crazy, like a big marshmallow with wheels.

Katherine circles the car manically. She's not satisfied. A group of four older guys I don't recognize walk by us and snicker at our prank, like it's kid stuff. One of them calls out that it's past our curfew. That only seems to work Katherine up more.

"This isn't good enough!" Katherine hisses, her eyes wide and darting around in desperation.

"Are you kidding?" Beth laughs. "He's going to be so pissed!"

Suddenly Katherine takes off running toward one of the nearby bungalows. Somehow I don't think her dad lives there, because it's decorated for Halloween with cardboard gravestones on the lawn and spiderwebs on the railings, like a family would do. The rest of us gather at the back bumper, unsure of what to do next.

"What's she doing?" Maria whispers.

"No clue," I say, burying my face in the sleeve of my borrowed cardigan sweater. The air smells disgustingly musty and minty from all the shaving cream we've squirted.

"We should get out of here before we get spotted," Beth says.

Katherine sprints up the bungalow stairs and grabs a huge pumpkin from the doorstep. It's a bit of a struggle to get the thing up in her arms — it must be at least twenty pounds — but once she does, she runs back over to the car in a full sprint.

"No, Katherine!" Beth shouts.

But Katherine can't hear us. She's screaming at the top of her lungs like some kind of warrior. When she gets close to her dad's car, she launches the pumpkin into the air. I try to steady my camera and time the shot right. It falls fast and crashes right down on the windshield, causing the glass to explode and pop into tiny glittering shards that reflect the streetlights.

"Oh my God!" Beth whispers.

Maria fumbles with her keys. "Geez, Katherine!"

Some people down the street turn and look our way. I hear shouting from behind us.

"Go, go, go!" Katherine leads the charge back to Maria's Volvo, stealing the keys along the way. Even though I'm practically crapping my pants with fear, I hold my camera over my shoulder and snap two more pictures behind me, praying that I capture some of this madness. Katherine dives into the driver's seat, and the rest of us cram into the back. No one is buckled up and my door is still open, but Katherine hits the gas so hard the engine roars. We speed off down the street and I fight to close the door against the wind of our escape.

The entire car is in silent shock, except for Katherine's breathless giggling. She fumbles to light herself a cigarette. She's not even looking at the road.

"Katherine, that was so not cool!" Maria shouts.

"Come on," she says. "That was a little bit cool."

"What the hell!" I say. "You could get us all in serious trouble!"

Beth doesn't say anything. She just climbs over Maria and me into the front seat.

Katherine's not at all fazed by my chastising. "How can you, of all people, not get it? Sometimes you gotta call people out or they'll think they can walk all over you forever."

And for the briefest, tiniest second, Beth's eyes catch mine in the visor mirror.

TWENTY-NINE

The snow seeped through my clothes, but I kept on smiling.

Beth and I were staring out of our igloo at her mother. A camera blocked most of her face, but you could still see her proud grin during her countdown to the flash.

We'd carved it out of a snowplow mound with small shovels Mr. Miller had gotten us from the garage. She and I built a tiny snow family to live inside with us. We'd been playing all afternoon.

I was so happy and proud of what we'd built, but I was also freezing. Every inch of me felt numb. I'd stopped even trying to wipe the snot dripping from my nose, because it just made my face wetter and colder. My snow pants and parka were far too small, leaving wide red bands of exposed skin around my wrists and ankles.

As much fun as I was having, I was ready to go home.

The flash popped, and I tried to suck in its warmth.

As if on cue, Mom's car pulled up to the curb. Maybe it was the ice, but she drove fast and erratic, almost crashing into the Millers' mailbox as she parked. She got out and raced toward me on a narrow shoveled-out path that led from the sidewalk up the front lawn to our igloo. She was still in her nursing scrubs and she wasn't wearing a coat. Her hair was wild and windblown.

"Isn't this amazing?" Mrs. Miller cooed, waving her hands around our snow dwelling. She told my mom she'd give her doubles of the pictures she'd taken.

My mom didn't say anything except, "Come on, Ruby. Let's go."

I was about to squeeze through our little entryway but Beth blocked my path. "Mom? Can Ruby sleep over? Or at least stay for dinner?"

Mom answered before the invitation was confirmed. "Sorry, Beth, but Ruby's going to have to come home now." Then she walked back to her car and got inside to wait for me.

I tried to leave the igloo again, but Beth was holding on to the hood of my parka. Her mouth fell into big frown, but I told her it was okay. That I'd see her tomorrow. Mom beeped the horn so I'd hurry up. Beth finally let me go.

I shivered the whole ride home. Mom said my lips were blue. She mumbled how the school should have tried to reach her if they'd called a snow day. And then, like an afterthought, she added how I could have frozen out there without snow clothes that fit me properly. Her hands wrung the steering wheel.

The house seemed asleep, even though Dad's truck was in the driveway. Usually he puttered around when he got home from work, fixing a faucet or attaching molding to the walls. But I couldn't hear him at all.

Mom helped me peel off my wet clothes and put me into my dry pajamas. She divided my wet hair into two pigtails and unrolled my sleeping bag out in front of the television set so I could watch *Annie* and keep warm at the same time.

THIRTY

I wake up with a start, nearly catapulting myself out of Beth's trundle bed. Maybe I was holding my breath while dreaming, because now I'm gasping for air. I press a blanket over my mouth to keep from waking everyone up. Maria and Katherine are sprawled on the floor in a pile of quilts. I step over them and sneak out of the room as quickly and quietly as I can.

I make it to the bathroom without a second to spare. I sit there, shivering on the toilet, peeing in little sputters. When I finish, I stand up and wash my hands with the nice-smelling soap Beth's mom always has near the sink. The Millers' towels are fluffy and soft, not scratchy and threadbare like ours. Right now, they're seasonal for Halloween, covered in little black cats and candy corn. They're almost too nice to wipe your hands on.

Then I flick off the lights. But instead of going back to Beth's room for a little more sleep, I sit on the side of the tub and try to hold still. Like maybe if I stopped moving, I could suspend time. But the sun slowly rises and burns orange through the window curtains. It's Saturday, the last day Jim is in town. Even though I made the decision not to see him, I still feel totally unsettled about the whole thing.

I focus on my dream. Beth and I built that igloo the day he left. Neither of us had any idea what was about to happen a few hours later. I wish I could have warned myself.

It's kind of twisted that Beth chose the photo of that day, of all days, to stick on her memory box. Maybe it has to do with the fact that our friendship went to the next level after that. I don't know.

If only I knew what was going to happen tomorrow. If not seeing Jim would be a thing I'd regret for the rest of my life, or something that would eventually go away again, like the hurt I felt when he left the first time.

I continue to sit on the edge of the tub for at least another hour, until Beth's dad knocks on the door because he has to get a shower. Even then, I still don't want to move because I don't know what to do.

Mrs. Miller has cooked a big birthday breakfast. She's made everything — waffles, eggs, bacon, home fries with tiny slices of green pepper mixed in, homemade blueberry muffins with little crumbly pieces on top. She's even squeezed fresh OJ. We all sit down at the long dining room table with Beth's mom and dad and Martha. Suzy has sent a bouquet of tiger lilies from college. They're in a big crystal vase at the center of the table.

I'm not sure who comes up with the idea, because I'm too busy pushing the eggs around on my plate to listen, but everyone goes around in a circle, sharing funny memories of Beth.

Mr. Miller is more than happy to go first. "When Beth was born, I got so excited making phone calls to my family that I ended up having some pretty major chest pain. So I went back to the delivery room to visit with Mom and asked one of the nurses to take my blood pressure, which was through the roof! I was this close to being admitted for heart palpitations."

"You're always trying to steal my thunder!" Mrs. Miller jokes as she lays another waffle down on her husband's plate. Then she goes on to tell a story about how when Beth was born, she was so bald that the doctor couldn't tell if it was her head or her butt coming out first.

Everyone laughs. Everyone but me.

Sharing time continues around the room, but I don't pay much attention. Until all the faces turn to face me. It's my turn.

Mrs. Miller's eyes flutter, because I've surely got a plethora of wonderful stories to share about Beth. But those aren't the things I'm thinking about right now.

I shrug my shoulders. "There are too many choices."

Everyone smiles and laughs politely. But they don't let me off the hook. Maria kicks my leg underneath the table and gives me a weird look.

So I think about that day I just dreamt about, that snow day.

"There was this one time Beth and I built a huge igloo and we played in it all day long. After a couple of hours in Suzy's snow pants and parka, I was soaking wet and ready to go home. But Beth refused to let me. She made Mrs. Miller bring us out hot chocolate and soup in mugs and we sat in there, freezing our butts off until it was nighttime."

Mrs. Miller brightens. "I think I have a picture of that! Hold on one second!" And she takes off for upstairs.

Beth stabs her fork into a mound of syrupy waffles. She doesn't look happy. "What made you think of that?"

"I don't know. I dreamt about it last night."

"Oh, yeah?" she says, like she doesn't quite believe me. Like I've got some ulterior motive or am trying to make her upset.

"Yeah," I say.

Mrs. Miller comes back after a few minutes empty-handed. "I know I gave your mother the double of that picture, Ruby, but I can't seem to find mine in the albums."

Beth doesn't say anything, even though she knows exactly where the picture is. It's on that box, in her room. And just the thought of it is making her very, very upset.

Beth's mom takes off her cats-eye glasses and cleans the lenses with the hem of her shirt. "Oh, well. I have tons to do today. Okay, girls, which one of you wants to pick up the cake and which one wants to help me make the Jell-O eyeballs?"

After a long day of running errands and making party plans, everyone's back in Beth's room, changing into their costumes and getting started with the birthday punch. I have to say, it's delicious. Beth has mixed some frozen fruit punch, mint leaves, ice, and Sprite with the raspberry vodka. I keep reminding myself to slow down but it's like I can't help but chug it.

Maria rubs lotion with tiny little sparkles in it on the length of the bare legs stretching out from under her tennis skirt. She looks great in her little outfit. Her phone buzzes next to her with yet another voice mail. It's been ringing all day, with kids asking what time they should come over and how much alcohol there's really going to be. She stopped picking it up an hour ago because she wanted to concentrate on her makeup. I bet the possibility of making out with Davey tonight has her all worked up.

I'm not sure exactly what Katherine's costume is supposed to be, but my best guess is some kind of prostitute zombie, because she's wearing lingerie and fishnets and has her makeup done all spooky and pale. She's perched on the windowsill of Beth's room, wafting the smoke of her cigarette outside. She balances a small mirror on her knee and lines her eyes in black pencil with her free hand.

Beth is missing — she wanted to get dressed in her mom's room, so she could surprise us all with her costume.

I'm still in my jeans and T-shirt, my costume stuffed into my book bag on the floor. I kind of don't feel like putting it on. So I pick up the phone and call my mom.

"Did anyone call me?"

"No, Ruby." She sounds really bummed, I guess left over from our last conversation. "Is something wrong? Do you want to come home?"

"No . . ." I say, but the *o* sound rises up like I really mean *yes*. I guess I was hoping that Charlie would have called. Though why would he? I didn't really give him much to say to make things better. He's moving and I made it clear that we were over. I'm just going to have to accept it and get over him. After all, we've known each other for barely a week. He's probably forgotten me by now.

Just then, there's a knock at the door. Beth's voice trills from the hallway, "Are you ready to see my costume?"

"Yes," Katherine and Maria say together. I quickly hang up and take another deep sip as the bedroom door swings open.

Beth's transformed that plain black slip from the thrift store into a proper flapper's dress right out of the 1920s. It's covered in swishy beads and swaying fringe. She's got on a short blond bob wig with an elastic black headband and a sparkly feather poking out. She removes a silver flask from her garter belt and sips from it.

"Oh, my God, you look amazing!" Maria coos. "I can't believe you made that!"

"Seriously, you look hot," Katherine says, getting ash all over the carpet.

"Wow" is all I can manage.

"When are you going to put on your costume?" she asks me.

"Now." I steal the flask from her hand.

The girls all coo over each other while I strip down in the corner between big hearty sips. When I bend over to pull up my knee socks, I almost fall down.

"Nice underwear!" Katherine yells at me.

Everyone thinks my costume looks great. But I'm just not feeling it. It's tight in all the most unflattering places, and I don't look comfortable at all. I should have never picked this as a costume.

Beth puts my hair up in pigtails, lends me her white beret, and applies some pink blush to the apples of my cheeks. As she's doing that, she takes notice of my badges.

"Whoa, what's all this?" she says, leaning forward to examine them closer. "These don't look like Girl Scout badges."

"They're not, exactly."

"What're they?" She points to one covered in black blobs.

"That's a Rorschach badge."

Her eyebrows rise up to her hairline. "A what?"

"Those stupid black blobs they hold up at the therapist and ask how they make you feel."

"And this one? With the squiggly lines?"

"It's a broken picture frame. A broken-family badge."

Beth wrinkles up her nose. She doesn't get it. But for all the reasons that I hate my costume, I'm pretty proud of the way my badges turned out. They feel like they fit me perfectly.

The front doorbell rings, and we all run to Beth's window to peek at who's here. It's a bunch of kids from the drama department dressed in these crazy elaborate Shakespearian costumes. Some of them even have on powdered wigs.

I guess it's party time.

THIRTY-ONE

The party is an enormous success. About fifty kids show up in costume, ready to dance, drink, and have a good time. Sure, a few of the boys come in plastic superhero masks made for little kids, but most people have gone all out. It's almost like how a teen party looks in the movies, except it's real. I walk around and take a few pictures, but mostly I'm just holding the camera up to my face so no one will talk to me.

The clock ticks away the night. With each passing hour, I grow more and more anxious about Jim. I thought Beth would be feeling nervous and worked up too, but she doesn't seem to have a care in the world. All she wants to focus on is her birthday. She's saying hi to everyone and accepting little presents and making sure cool music is always on the stereo. Every time I spot her through the crowd, she's gulping from her plastic cup. She's always on the opposite side of the garage from me. It seems almost purposeful, and she's been acting all weird toward me since our conversation this morning. There are a few minutes when I can't even find her in the crowd.

Maria isn't talking to me either. Davey did show up, dressed like a mummy. I'm guessing they made their relationship official tonight, since the white cloth around his mouth is tainted red from her lipstick. I want to be happy for Maria, but I can't. I know it's crazy, but I kind of even hate her a little bit.

The person I can't seem to shake is Katherine. She's walking around behind me, leaning in and whispering insults like how stupid some kid in her history class looks in his Zorro outfit, and how some freshman girl in a Goldilocks wig has been dancing like a slut all over the boys. It's beyond annoying.

"Can you please stop?" I say, lifting the cup to my mouth.

She recoils, genuinely upset. "Why are you still mad at me? We didn't get arrested or anything. My dad obviously didn't call the cops. So what's your problem? You think I'm trying to steal your best friend or something?"

"That's insane." Why does Katherine care what I think anyway?

"Well, what then? I feel like you hate me."

I sip my cup until it's empty. "That's not true."

"Then prove it. Let's have a cigarette." Katherine knocks into me, sort of playful.

"I don't smoke."

"Shut up." She extends the pack of cigarettes in my direction.

I can't help but think of Jim, the smoker. He's probably having a cigar right now, watching the clock tick down like I am. I take one of Katherine's and bite down on the filter, like I'm tough. And we walk out the side door together into the night.

Katherine flicks her lighter a few times and, once she has a flame, cups it carefully near the tip of my face. It makes my nose feel warm. "Suck it in slowly," she says. She lights up her own, puffs, and blows out a long steady stream before I can even switch the cigarette from my right hand to my left. It doesn't make holding it feel any less awkward, though.

I draw in a shallow breath and hold the smoke in my mouth. Some leaks down the back of my throat and I cough like an idiot. Katherine doesn't make fun of me, though, which is surprising. Instead she says, "Everyone does that their first time."

I take another tiny puff and quickly blow it into the sky. "You really like the taste of these things?" I ask her.

"No." She takes another long drag.

"Jim is a smoker," I tell her.

"My dad too," she says. "He's also an asshole."

"Jim is too."

She takes in a deep breath, her first without the cigarette perched on her lips, and tips her head back to look at the stars. "But I still feel bad about what I did to his car."

"Really?" I'm surprised to hear it.

Katherine laughs. "Why is that so hard to believe? I think I've probably said 'I'm sorry' to you like a million times since we started hanging out." She pauses for a deep drag. "But I still feel like it's good to be impulsive. Sometimes you've just got to do and say what's on your mind, no matter who you're going to piss off." She leans back toward the garage door, making sure no one is coming. "Did those pictures that you took come out?"

"They came out okay."

"Can I have one?"

"Yeah, sure. You can have them all, if you want."

We don't talk for the rest of the smoke. I don't take any more puffs. I just watch the length of ash grow and fall to the ground.

"You survived your first cigarette," Katherine says to me. "Now you've earned yourself a cigarette-smoking badge." She takes her butt and snaps it between her fingers, sending it flying off into the yard. "Here," she says, and twists my fingers into the same shape.

I snap my fingers like she tells me to, but the lit butt comes flying back into my shirt. It just bounces right off though.

Katherine laughs. "Smooth."

"Whatever," I say with a smile.

"So we're cool now?" she asks me.

And I nod.

My throat is killing me, so I head into the house for a glass of water. Beth's mom is at the kitchen window, peering out through the curtains at the garage. I straighten up and act as sober as I can. I hope I don't reek of cigarette smoke.

"Is everyone having a good time out there, Ruby?" she asks me.

"Yeah. It's really fun."

"How about Beth? Is she having a good time?"

"Oh, yeah, definitely."

"I'm glad." Mrs. Miller lets the curtain fall. "Is everything okay with her lately?"

"I think so. Why?"

"No reason. I guess she seems a little bit down in the dumps the last few days. She's spent lots of time in her room, working on her costume, of course, but . . . I don't know, she just hasn't been acting very Bethy, you know?"

I shrug my shoulders because I don't really know what to say.

She shakes her head and drops the subject. "Ruby, you must be freezing out there without a coat. I think I saw yours on Beth's bed."

"I'm fine, actually. It's pretty warm with everyone inside dancing." Then I think about Beth's room and that memory box with our picture on top. I want to know what's inside of it. "But maybe I'll get it just in case I go hang out outside again."

It's weird being up in Beth's room when she's not here. It feels dirty and sneaky, but not enough to stop me. I go straight back into her closet and look for the memory box on the shelf. But it's gone.

She knew I was going to look for it.

One second later and I'm tearing the room apart. I drag her mattress off the frame, pull the clothes out of her drawers. The whole time, I know it's a terrible idea to be doing this, and I'll definitely have some explaining to do, but I can't stop. When I kick over her wastebasket, the memory box tumbles out from underneath a pile of lipstick-stained tissues and fabric scraps.

I'm shaking as I hold it. I flip it open, and find my dad's letter right on top. Under that are a bunch of Beth's memories. Like the plastic necklaces we got from Red Lobster, a love note from Pete Southern, a poem she wrote for the school's journal, and the ticket stub from the time we went to our first concert in Cleveland. And then I see something I wouldn't have ever predicted.

A key.

It's the one to my old house.

THIRTY-TWO

When I come back down to the garage, I am shaking so hard my teeth chatter.

The entire party is screaming the "Happy Birthday" song. They are all gathered around Beth, like she's some kind of celebrity. Everyone's pretty drunk, especially Beth. She keeps leaning over, falling ever so slightly against Maria and Katherine, who flank her at the birthday-cake table.

I'm in shock that they're already singing. It's like Beth didn't even care that I was missing. I press my lips together as tightly as I can, protesting the entire thing. The song ends, Beth blows out the candles, and everyone cheers before getting back to the dance floor. As the crowd disperses, Beth looks at me, then up at the clock. It's almost midnight. She adjusts her wig and the corners of her mouth turn up the littlest bit.

I step forward and shove a wrapped present in her hand. "Happy birthday."

She takes it apprehensively. "Thanks."

"Open it," I say.

She does. Gently and slowly, as if the wrapping paper was expensive and not the comics page from last Sunday's newspaper. I can tell she's impressed. She flips the pages of the Polaroid flipbook and watches as I smile big, wide, and normal for her. I get a weird satisfaction in her happiness, like this proves that I really am a good friend, one who can make the perfect gift for her. Too bad she doesn't deserve it.

"This is awesome," she says softly. "Seriously. It's just what I wanted."

When she looks back up at me, her face changes. It gets tight. The gold key reflects in her eyes. I'm dangling it in front of her face.

Beth turns bright red. She tries to lead me away from the party guests, over to the near-empty punch bowl that's in the corner, but she's stumbly and buzzed. I grind my heels, because after all this time, I'm ready to have it out and I don't care who's here to see it. But she ultimately wrestles me to the back side of the door, in a small dark shadow next to the fridge.

"I spent all week trying to tell myself that there was no way you'd keep this from me." I hold the letter up to her face, so close it touches her nose.

Beth pushes it away. The paper almost rips. Her mouth is wide open. "You went digging through my room? Through my personal stuff?"

"I wouldn't have had to if you hadn't purposefully hidden that box from me!"

She shakes her head back and forth, like she can't believe it. "That was my memory box! You had no right to look in it!"

My hands fall to my sides but then immediately spring back up. I can't believe she's trying to turn this around on me. "Yeah, with that picture on top of the day my dad left? What a cherished memory for you to hold on to!"

"Sorry I care about you, okay? Sorry I don't want you to get hurt." She is so defiant.

"Oh, please. You just love telling me what to do. You do it to everyone! You tell Katherine to bury her feelings about her dad. You tell Maria to get over Davey. You think you can go around and dictate how everyone should live their lives. Well, I'm not letting you run mine anymore."

"Right, Ruby. Like I'm such a bad person. All I did was try to help you, keep you positive and give you advice *when you asked me for it.* Did I ask to be drawn into your whole family drama? No. Was it fun for me to have to help pick up the pieces of your life? I don't think so." She rolls her eyes. "Yeah, I'm such a monster. Give me a break."

"Is that what you call advice?" The words pop out fast and hard like punches. "Don't you mean *Listen to what I say or else?* Because that's what you basically said to me in the library." My hands clench into fists. "You're not supposed to tell me what to do. It's my life. If I want to see my dad, you can't stop me!" I swear to God I'll hit her if she tries to stop me.

Beth sucks in air through her gaping mouth. Then she leans forward, throwing her arm up on my shoulder. She's not even the slightest bit afraid of me. Her eyes get narrow and mean. "If you really wanted to see Jim, Ruby, if you knew about his letter all along, why didn't you just go? Why did you need my permission?"

I take a step back, unclench my fists, and steady myself against the wall. A few couples on the dance floor have noticed us fighting and angle themselves for a better view. "I know I didn't need your permission. I was hoping that you'd eventually come clean about it! I trusted that you were my friend and that you would tell me the truth! And what do I get for giving you the benefit of the doubt? My dad's probably gone by now! And I'll never get to see him again." Then I start to cry, right there.

"Stop trying to make me sound like a bad friend," Beth screams back into my wet face. She rips off her feather headband and throws it on the ground. "I have a good reason for not telling you!"

I wipe my eyes and stare at her so hard I think she might spontaneously combust from the heat. Beth is the most insensitive, self-obsessed person in the history of the world. How could I have not noticed before? "Right, I know all your reasons. You hate my dad. He's a total screwup. He left me and my mom. I got it. But he's still my dad. Not Jim. My dad!"

Beth is so frustrated, she's practically jumping up and down. She lets out a big exasperated groan. "No! That's not it! I wish that were it, for your sake."

"Then what? Explain it to me. And tell me why it is exactly that you have the key to my old house? Because that's just creepy."

Beth opens her mouth to yell again, but she closes it again before any words come out. Her eyes look around the room at all the faces staring at us. Someone turns the music off.

Maria runs up to us, dragging Davey along with her. "What's going on?"

Katherine comes up behind me. She pulls the letter out of my hand and scans it quickly. I'm too stunned to stop her.

The blood drains from Beth's face, and when she looks back at me, she's pale as a ghost. "I walked in on your mom with some other guy that day we built the igloo. I didn't want you to have to see it, so I took your stupid key. And I've been keeping it secret so you wouldn't have to know that it was your mom's fault this happened in the first place." She bends over, picks up her headband, and hangs it on the doorknob.

"Shut up," I say, gasping for breath like someone's holding a pillow over my face. I take a step back. And another.

Maria drops Davey's hand and reaches for me. "Ruby, wait. Don't go."

Katherine guides Maria's arm away from me. She folds up the note and places it in my clammy hand.

Beth turns her back to me. I take off running.

THIRTY-THREE

Beth was at a doctor's appointment.

I watched though holes in the paper snowflakes taped to our classroom window as the school playground was quickly blanketed in snow. Before the end of the lesson, the principal came over the loudspeaker and announced that school would be closing early. I remember being shocked because you could still see parts of the blacktop under the trees and benches. But the big, fat, white flakes showed no signs of stopping, just like the news reports had predicted.

When I came home, Beth was shivering underneath our big oak tree in her pink parka. She'd heard about our snow day on the car radio on her way home and came to meet me at my house so we could make a snowman or an igloo or something. But my mom wasn't home from work yet, she said. So Beth told me I should just come over her house.

I wanted to change into my snow pants and boots. Beth was tugging on me and insisted that I borrow snow clothes at her house. I shook my head. I was way taller than her or even her older sister

Suzy. It would only take a second to duck inside. But when I lifted up the rock underneath the garden spigot, the spare key that was always underneath had gone missing.

"Weird," I said, because that had never happened before. I fell to my knees, melting the light coating of snow with my hot palms to see if the key might be in arm's reach of its normal hiding spot.

"Come on!" Beth said, pulling my collar so hard that I fell backward.

"Okay, okay," I said.

As we neared the end of my street, my dad's truck appeared from around the corner. He slowed down, and I waved and smiled. I told him mom wasn't home and I was going over to Beth's. I told him the key was missing.

"Really?" He glanced over our shoulders at the dark, empty house.

I looked to Beth for confirmation of my story. She was making the strangest, most apologetic face ever, right at my dad. Like she knew something terrible was about to happen.

But instead of stopping it, Beth took off for the corner, running as quickly as she could.

THIRTY-FOUR

Riding your bike is dangerous when you're crying. My feet keep slipping off the pedals and I'm steering all wobbly and crazy down the middle of the street. The front tire dips into a dark pothole and I lose my balance. I skid out into a parked car, nearly falling off the seat, but manage to right myself before I hit the pavement. The inside of my calf scrapes the bike chain, leaving behind an oily gash.

I've decided not to go right to the Holiday Inn, even though he might be gone by the time I get there. Maybe it's because I'm scared. But I have to make a stop first. I have to hear it from her.

Mom is in her bedroom. I can tell by the way the light from the television flashes and flickers through the lace curtains. I crash through the back door and round the corner to her.

"Ruby?" she calls out.

I nudge her door open with my foot. She's lying underneath her comforter, her hair up in a towel. I can't see the television from where I'm standing, but the way the music is swelling and all violiny, I know she's watching one of those stupid romance movies.

"Ruby? Are you okay?" She cocks her head to the side. "What happened to your leg? You're bleeding!" But instead of jumping out of bed and racing to my side, like the nurse in her should want to do, she pulls up the covers, like she's afraid of me or something.

"Is there anything you want to tell me, Mom?"

Her eyes narrow. "Like what? What do you mean?"

I lean against the doorway, trying to look really casual and calm and in control. "Okay. Let me rephrase the question. Is there anything you think you *should* tell me?" I watch her and wait for her answer, expecting to see her squirm under her covers and grow all anxious.

But she doesn't. Mom pats her hand around her bed sheets, looking for the remote. She lowers the volume, but keeps the television on. "It sounds like you already know."

Her cool demeanor is really pissing me off. Shouldn't she be more ashamed? Sad? Apologetic? "That you're a cheater? Yeah, I know. I know all about you." My voice quivers. "And I know that it was your fault he left us."

Mom shakes her head, defiant. "It wasn't my fault." She says it quick and confident.

I scratch the back of my neck, which is hot and itchy. I'd thought I was going to catch Mom off guard and have to force her to talk about this, but she seems weirdly prepared for our conversation. "Why are you even bothering to defend yourself? Beth saw you with someone else! She used the spare key and saw everything! And if you honestly thought you weren't guilty, you would have told me about it a long time ago."

"I didn't think you'd understand. I thought you would judge me." She leans her head back and rubs her eyes. "And that's exactly what you're doing."

"What do you expect me to think, Mom?" I stamp my feet hard onto the floor. Her collection of little perfume bottles tinkles like a wind chime.

"This wasn't about you, Ruby. I kept you out of it because this had nothing to do with you."

"It has everything to do with me! You drove Dad away! You made me feel sorry for you. All the times you seemed sad and lonely were just lies and ways to manipulate me! But I won't let you do that anymore."

"I never tried to manipulate you."

"You know, Dad's in town, right now. At the Holiday Inn. He's been there since my birthday. He sent me a letter and a whole box of pictures and stuff. Stuff so I'd come and see him. But I didn't go, because I wasn't going to forgive him for leaving us. Only now I know you're the one who caused this. You're the one who's kept me from having a relationship with him! You've ruined everything!" I pivot and turn my back to her. "I hate you!" I don't even feel the least bit sorry.

She tries to call after me. She wants to explain her side. But now that I've told her what I had to, I just want to get as far away from my mom as I can.

THIRTY-FIVE

The illuminated Holiday Inn sign erases the nearby stars from the sky around it. It's so bright and magnetic. My legs whirl in a circle like a machine, propelling me closer and closer and closer. I lean into a turn and climb the big hill. I have to pedal standing up to keep my momentum. Beth's white beret flies off my head and into the middle of the road behind me. I don't even think about turning around for it.

I coast into the hotel parking lot dripping with sweat and barely able to breathe. I fling my bike into one of the bushes near the main entrance and run into the lobby.

It's much quieter inside than the last time I was here. Partly because the piped-in classical music is shut off. The lobby is pretty deserted and all the bright lights have been dimmed.

There's a young guy sitting behind the front desk. He doesn't look as polished as the older man who worked the day shift. He has a nose ring and a stubbly goatee. The collar of his button-up is open and his tie is knotted loosely around his neck. He's reading a motorcycle magazine and has a sandwich spread out on the counter. He barely glances in my direction as he reaches for a handful of potato chips, so I just run right past him and head for the stairwell.

The carpet on the fourth floor is the color of wheat. I pass room after room. Each one has a huge window that faces the center of the hotel with thick curtains to block out the light of the hallway. Everybody seems to be asleep. My courage drains like bathwater in a tiny little spiral at the bottom of my shoes. What if I can't wake him up? Should I just crash in the hallway until morning? Or should I pound on his door until he answers? How badly do I actually want this? And what if he's already gone?

I stop a few feet ahead of his room. His window curtains are pulled open. I see a desk light on and I think I can hear his television. I stop to peek over the railing at the lobby and the vertigo nearly makes my knees give out.

When I turn back, I see my dad inside his room, packing up his stuff into a large duffel bag on top of his unmade bed. Just like old times.

He looks up and spots me, an overgrown Girl Scout lurking in the hallway. For a moment, I don't think he even recognizes me. But he tosses the sweater he's only half folded off to the side and moves to the door to let me in.

"Hi," I say, my bottom lip quivering.

He smiles in a shy way, like he's unsure if that's an appropriate response to our first real meeting, and holds the door open for me. I step inside and take a seat on an overstuffed lounge chair. The room reeks of smoke so bad it makes me cough. The ashtray in front of me is packed with stubbed-out cigar butts and flecks of ash seem to cover every surface. He sits on the corner of the bed.

The quiet makes the air in the room heavy and hard to

breathe. My eyes leap all over him, not stopping on one detail too long to be caught staring. I observe him in small pieces — a flannel shirt, a white tube sock, a scratchy beard, a pockmark on the side of his neck, a tuft of hair poking out of his ear. We're both chewing on our fingers. I wonder what he sees when he looks at me.

"Can I use the bathroom?" I ask, suddenly jumping up out of the chair.

"Sure, sure." He darts into the bathroom and grabs his toiletries, like his razor and toothbrush, and drops them all into a hotel towel. Then he folds up the corners like a hobo sack. "I don't think there are any fresh towels left, but I can call down to the lobby if you need one."

"That's okay."

I go in, shut the door, and stare at myself in the mirror. I look like total crap. Eye makeup is smeared all over my face. The corners of my mouth are red from Beth's party punch. I wash my face and my hands. There aren't any clean towels, just a pile of dirty ones on the floor. I use a big wad of toilet paper to dry myself off and then a second one to get some of the dirt and dried blood out of my cut. I attempt to straighten my shirt, but it's all lumpy and weird and wrinkled and there's really no hope for me to look anything but a big mess. There are a few drops of mouthwash left in the tiny bottle, so I swish some of that around. I try to figure out what it is, exactly, that I want to say to him. Or what I'm hoping to hear. Then over my shoulder I spot a newspaper on the floor near the toilet, open to an advertisement for tools on sale at the local hardware shop. It feels weirdly intimate for me to see something like that. So I walk back into the room entirely unprepared.

He's returned to packing, but stops as soon as I sit back down in my seat. He lights up another cigar. I think about asking him not to smoke but I chicken out. After all, this is his room. He takes a big drag while I say, "I'm sorry I waited until tonight to come here." I think about explaining how I never really got his letter in the first place but it all seems like too insane a story to tell at this point.

His lips part and a cloud of smoke leaks out. "That's okay, Rubes. Better late than never, right?"

I nod my head even though I'm not really sure. But I hope so.

"I've thought about calling on you for a while now," he continues. My mind briefly wanders. Does he mean six years is a while? Or three? Or one? Or a few months? "But it's the kind of thing where, after so much time has passed, you don't really know how the phone works anymore. You have no idea what to say."

"I still don't know what to say to you," I admit.

He shakes his head. "I've never been good at things like this. Feelings and stuff."

"Me neither." I chuckle a little bit. He does too. Our laughs sound the same. Quiet and nervous. Mom always tries to fight through awkwardness and pretend like everything's fine. It's exhausting to play her game. But Dad and I both know this is weird, and it's kind of a relief.

"Why are you here?" I ask.

He smiles in a shy way and reaches for a nearby ashtray that he balances on the inside of his foot. "When I happened to be passing through Ohio, I thought to myself, *It's now or never.* So I pulled over, took a look at the phone book in Dodie's, and found you." His eyes travel down to the floor. "I'm sorry for ruining your party. I felt really bad about that."

"It's okay, Dad."

"Did you get the box?"

He looks at me all expectantly. The same way he did when he held out those flowers for me on my birthday. "Yes." I don't know what else to say to him. It was just a bunch of random junk.

He smiles. "Good. I think you can learn a lot about a person by seeing what they keep in the top drawer of their dresser."

All I keep in my top drawer is underwear. I don't know what that says about me. "I thought you and Mom looked young in the pictures."

"We were. That was part of the problem."

"That and her cheating," I say. He looks up at me, surprised. "I just found out that tonight, Dad. If I had known, I definitely would have come sooner. I thought the whole divorce and everything was your fault. But now I understand why you left."

I thought maybe that would make him happy, but instead of smiling, he looks at me kind of funny, like I'm not getting it. "I couldn't forgive her, Ruby. I gave up too much for her to do that to me." His words sting. I guess I have a confused look on my face or something, because he shifts his weight, clears his throat, and tries to start over. "I wasn't ready when she told me she was pregnant, I wasn't ready to buy a house, and ten years after you came along, I still wasn't ready to be a father." He smashes out the cigar tip in the ashtray. "It was just the out I needed. We both needed it."

My whole body tenses up. He's talking about everything like it was just him and Mom. But there was someone else involved.

"I wish I'd had an out. Things were really awful for me. I don't know if you know that or not. But they were."

We look at each other for a long time then, like a staring contest that neither of us wants to lose. Eventually, he stands up and then so do I. But instead of coming over to hug me or to do something dadlike, he grabs his bags and we both walk out of the hotel room.

"I'm very happy you're here," he says over his shoulder.

I run a few steps to catch up. "Really?"

"Yes, really," he says, like it should be obvious to me. "I would have felt bad if you never came at all."

My face tightens up. There's that deserving, entitled tone again. "Well, what did you do all week? Did you see old friends or something?"

"I don't know anyone here, Ruby. This isn't my home."

"Where's home then?"

"I've been transferred to another park up in Maine. I'm going to be manning a remote ranger station up in Acadia National Park. I'll be driving all night and day to get there, and I start on Monday." He glances back at me. "If it weren't for that, I'd spend tomorrow with you."

"Oh. Doesn't it get lonely?"

"I like it. I like being on my own."

"That's how you are?" I say, squinting my eyes.

He nods. "How are you?"

"I'm not that way," I say slowly, even though I'm still very much alone. So alone it makes it hard to swallow.

I follow him silently out to the parking lot and watch him load the blue pickup truck again. That's when I start to cry.

Dad tries to hug me, but he only uses one arm. I cry harder.

"I'd say we could exchange e-mail addresses, but I don't have a computer." He rubs his beard. "I can write you when I get there, though I'll probably be really very busy for the first few months getting settled and everything."

A huge bubble of snot bursts out of my nostril, but I don't even care. This is not how I hoped this would go. Not even close.

"Please stop crying," he says softly. "Wasn't this a nice visit?"

I sniffle and look around the parking lot. He randomly shows back up after six years of nothing. And after a fifteen-minute chat, he expects insta-relationship and warm fuzzies? "Not really, Dad. I mean . . . I don't know."

He shakes the change in his pocket. "Remember, I waited here all week for you. It didn't have to be rushed like this."

His words hang in the air. He wants it, so long as he doesn't have to work for it. But I worked very hard to be here, to see him. All he did was take an unexpected exit off the highway. "What do you want? A medal?" My tears dry up and I get angry. I can't even look at him.

"No, I don't want a medal. I just thought things would be different, now that you're older. I thought you'd understand."

"Understand what?"

"Understand me. That I wasn't ready to be a father."

All I'm hearing is that he took advantage of Mom's mistake to shirk his responsibilities to us. She was wrong to cheat on him, but what he did wasn't right, either. "And are you ready now?" I'm pretty raw and emotional. "Is that why you came here? You want to be my dad now?"

His face begs for sympathy. "I don't know. I guess I'm still trying to figure that out." But it's like he already knows the answer, because he gets in the driver's side, closes the door, and lowers the window halfway. "I will write you. I'll figure out something to say to you and write you."

This is it. This is all I'm going to get.

"Wait, Dad?" I wipe my face on my sleeve and rummage through my book bag to find my camera. Then I lean against the truck, hold out my arm, try to fit both of us in the shot, and pull the trigger. But my Polaroid doesn't make a sound.

"Let me have a look," he says, unrolling the window the rest of the way and reaching for it. I hand it over. "I used to have one like this and it always got stuck." He pops open the front hatch and fiddles with something inside. "You like taking pictures?"

"I guess, yeah."

"Me too. I've been documenting some tree diseases for the service." He flips the latch closed. "Try again."

I do. And it works.

"Rubes," he says. "At least remember that I tried, okay?"

And then he rolls up his window and drives away.

I pedal out of the hotel parking lot without anywhere to go. I don't have any of the answers or the closure that I wanted. In fact, my whole world is wide open. Wide open and empty. Before I can stop myself, I'm on my way to my old house.

It's too late for there to be any trick-or-treaters left out. I ride boldly in the middle of the street. Make a left, and a right.

Thudding bass grows in the distance. Teddy's party. As I get closer to his house, the music gets louder. I can see the shadows of people in the windows, bumping and grinding into each other. There's a person in the driveway, sitting on the stone wall, throwing rocks into the street. He's dressed in a huge cardboard square. He's cut out arm holes and leg holes and painted the whole thing to look like a cookie box. The perfect companion to my Girl Scout costume.

"Ruby! Hey!"

But I ride right by Charlie. I skid to a stop in front of my old house.

It's so beautiful, so well taken care of. I look up into the orange oak tree. A small wooden tree house is nestled in the branches.

"Ruby!" Charlie's voice calls out. He's awkwardly shuffling as fast as he can down the street in his cookie costume.

I toss my bike down and climb up the rope ladder to the tree house. As I disappear inside the branches, my tears flow more and more.

"What are you doing?" he calls out from the ground.

I peer past the pillowcase tacked up to the door frame and hiss "Go away!"

But he doesn't. He follows me up.

The tree house is dark and shadowy and really cramped. I have to slouch to keep my head from scraping against the wood ceiling. There's a pile of sticks and leaves in the corner, some Army men lined up across the windowsill, and a rubber-band gun with no ammo.

"What happened?" Charlie asks me, as he climbs in.

"I'm so messed up. For nothing. Over nothing." I retreat to the corner opposite him, even though I'm still in arm's reach.

"C'mere," he says folding me into his arms, crinkling the cardboard of his big cookie box. I try to wriggle out, but it's no use. He's holding me too tight. So I just cry and cry and cry.

THIRTY-SIX

I wake up inside a square of sunlight that shines through the window of the tree house. As yellow and bright as it is, it provides no warmth. The icy breeze is strong through the trees and squeaks through the million cracks between the wood beams. My Girl Scout costume is damp and so is the plywood floor underneath me. I shiver.

Two thermal-covered arms squeeze me until I am still again. I look up from the lap where I am comfortably lying, despite the general uncomfortableness of where I am. Charlie is asleep, his back up against the side of the tree house. His crumpled and dented cookie costume is across from us in a corner. His fingers are twitching in tiny movements, like he's typing on an invisible typewriter. I guess because he's freezing too. His sweatshirt is draped over my bare legs.

I nudge him gently. His eyes flutter open. "Hey," he says with a tired voice. And gives me a squeeze.

"Hey," I say back.

I notice the key in my hands when I push myself up off the floor. I guess I've been squeezing it all night because my palm is marked by red flecks that match the toothy grooves. It's all tender and sore.

"Do you know what time it is?" I ask.

He checks his watch. "Almost nine-thirty. Are you hungry? We could go get some breakfast or something."

My stomach is empty but I'm not hungry. "I should probably go home." I stand up and dust my dirty, wrinkly self off. I can't even imagine how bad I must look right now.

Charlie gets up too. He moves really slow and quiet as he dusts off his jeans, like he doesn't want to disturb me or distract me from whatever I might be thinking about.

I move over to the window and stare down at my old house. It's a really nice house. I'll probably be sad forever that it's not where I live anymore.

Charlie creeps up behind me. He puts his hands on my shoulders and leads me away from the window and into a shadow. "We should probably keep out of sight." He pulls a leaf out of my hair. Instead of throwing it on the ground, he tucks it into his pocket. Which is totally weird and sweet and very Charlie.

My heart races. "I can't believe you're going to move," I say. Tears well up in my eyes.

"It's not going to be for a while."

"But that's what I mean. How can I be with someone I know is going to leave me?" I'm full-on crying now.

He wipes my face with the sleeve of his thermal. It's really soft and smells like dryer sheets. It's like the most perfect tissue. "I don't know."

"And I can't just forget it either, Charlie. I've tried that before and it doesn't work."

He wraps up my hands in his and blows on them to keep them warm. "I don't know what to say, Ruby. It totally sucks. I know that."

I take a bunch of deep breaths and wrap my arms around Charlie as tightly as I can. We climb down the tree house ladder, him first, me second, and we lock hands at the bottom. Charlie tries to lead me to the street and away from my house, but I pull him harder up the front lawn. We walk over to the front door and kneel down in the grass together. Then I pick up a rock and I put my old house key back underneath.

"What now? Where are you going?"

I don't know what's going to happen between us. Well, in a way I guess I do. But it's not like I'm my dad and I'm caught in a situation I don't want to be in. I'm not looking for an out. I want to be *in*.

"I'm going home," I say. I tell Charlie I'll call him later. And I mean it.

THIRTY-SEVEN

When I get home, Beth is sitting on my front stairs. Her body droops like a rag doll and she's playing catch with a half-empty water bottle. She's dressed in grungy jeans, a stained sweatshirt that she likes to sleep in, and a pair of navy-blue Vans. Her wavy hair seems flatter than normal, I guess from being tucked underneath her wig all night. Traces of last night's eye makeup hide in the folds of her lids. She doesn't say hello to me, or even make eye contact as I walk past her. She keeps her eyes locked on my peacoat and my book bag, lying next to her.

I reach up on the awning and grab the spare key. I slide it into the lock, but stop turning a second before it clicks over. Even though I'm totally exhausted and emotionally drained, Beth and I will have to have it out sooner or later. Even if we're never going to be friends again, someone has to say as much, to make it official. And if that's how things are going to be, I'd rather have it happen sooner than later. I never want to be suspended in the limbo of non-decision again. It's like torturing yourself on purpose.

I shuffle back down the stairs and lean against the railing. "Hey."

"Hi." She wrings her hands and keeps her eyes off me. "So you saw him?"

"Yup."

"Are you okay? How'd it go?"

I tip my head back and look at the sky. She hasn't exactly earned the right to hear the story. But if we're going to have it out, I guess I can't hold anything back. So I sit down on the stairs next to her. "It wasn't great. He expected a lot. Way more than he deserved."

"Oh." She looks at me briefly, then back at the ground. "Listen, I know you probably don't want to hear it, but I'd still like to explain why I did what I did." She stares out at the front lawn. "Though maybe *I'm* expecting more than I deserve." She laughs a little bit.

I don't. "Listen, Beth, I want to say something to you first. You're not going to convince me that what you did to me wasn't wrong. So if you're planning on being all defensive and self-righteous, like you were acting last night, then just forget it."

There's a chance Beth might blow up at me again for saying something like that to her. Instead she just takes a big deep breath, like she's about to dive underwater. "You know, my party pretty much broke up right after you left. I sent everyone home and spent the rest of the night buried underneath my comforter. Katherine and Maria stayed awhile to help pick up the mess you made of my room. Both of them were pretty intent on telling me how wrong I was for doing what I did to you. Like, over and over again. A taste of my own medicine, I guess."

"You needed them to tell you that what you did was wrong?"

"No. I've known it all along."

"I don't know if that makes things better or worse." I shake my head.

Beth rubs her own shoulders, wincing a bit. "It makes it worse. I know it does."

This conversation isn't going anywhere, and I'm getting more and more tired by the second. I pick up my peacoat and wrap it around my shoulders. Maybe I should just go inside.

Beth wrings her hands. "Can I say one thing, though?"

"Sure."

"I kept the key to your old house because I was eventually going to tell you everything. And that igloo picture was a reminder that I owed it to you to take care of you through everything until I could tell you the truth."

I shake my head. "You didn't owe me anything. You should have just told me."

"No, you're wrong." Her eyes well up and her cheeks get red. "I should have done something. I could have rung your doorbell or asked your dad to drive us to my house or even yelled your name really loud so that maybe your mom would hear me and stop and she wouldn't have gotten caught."

"I don't even care about that, Beth."

"Well, you should!" She chews on her fingernail. "I always told myself that being a good friend to you somehow made up for what I'd done. But deep down I knew that I could have fixed everything if I'd just reacted differently." Beth completely breaks down, tears running all over her face.

"But how were you going to justify letting my dad leave town without telling me? I would have never seen him again if I didn't find that letter! And, coincidentally, you'd also never have to own up to anything you did."

Beth puffs up. "You said that you didn't *want* to see him again, remember? I thought I was helping you. He did leave you and your mom, after all."

I stare her right in the face. "But that's not your call to make. I need to know that you're behind me, no matter what I want to do."

"Right. I know." We sit quietly for a few seconds. She sniffles and wipes her face with her sweatshirt sleeves. "God, I'm just like the worst friend in the whole world, huh?" And then she explodes in tears all over again.

"I mean, you messed up. The key isn't as bad as the letter to me, but it all really sucks."

Her whole body shakes as she holds back tears long enough to say something. "Do you ever think we'll be okay again? Like how we used to be?" Her neck twitches, like she wants to look at me but doesn't have the courage.

She really is sorry for what she's done and all the mistakes she's made. But everything between us has changed because of what she did. There's no ignoring it.

Maybe that's a good thing, though.

I take a chunk of her waves in my hand and separate them into little strands.

I'm not going to need Beth in the same way anymore. But I'm still going to need her. And she's going to need me too.

THIRTY-EIGHT

Mom is waiting for me in the living room. She's got the box from my dad on her lap and she's flipping through the photos. I guess she went into my room and found it.

"Mom, I —" I stammer. I have no idea what I should say to her. But she pats the couch cushion next to her. So I just sit down.

She flips to a photo of herself with long hair wearing a pretty flowered dress. She shakes her head. "It's hard for me to look at this stuff." I try to close up the box, but she swats my hand away. "I want to jump into this picture and warn the old me." She sighs and flips to the next photo. "The stupidest thing I ever did was to try and protect you from what I'd done, Ruby. I should have been honest." She takes a deep breath and puts the photos away. "I'm going to be better with that. We need to be better about that."

"I should have told you he was still in town. But I was afraid it would hurt you," I say. She smiles at me, but I can't bear to look at her. "I saw him last night. It was really weird."

She rubs something off my cheek. Dirt, probably. "I was actually sad when you ran out like that on your birthday. I thought it might be good for you to see him."

"Weren't you afraid he would tell me that you cheated?"

"I was, initially. But there was also a part of me that knew it would come out someday. I even planned to tell you myself, that night we carved the pumpkins." She brushes my bangs off my forehead. "But I lost my courage."

"It wasn't your fault he left, Mom. He was looking for an escape. He didn't want to make things work."

"Ruby, as much as I had come to terms with what I'd done and the ultimate effect it had on my marriage, I still felt responsible for all the pain you had to go through. I guess closing myself off from everything and everyone was my way of repenting."

"All this time I thought you were still in love with him. And that's why you never dated anyone else."

She smiles. "That would make sense."

"Who was it? The guy you were with."

"Nobody special. Just an old friend I'd known in high school."

"Was it the guy you lost your virginity to?"

Her face flushes red. "What? How did you know about that?"

"I read your journal when we moved. I wanted to know about you, Mom."

She pats my legs and laughs. "Shouldn't that be the other way around?"

I let my head fall onto her shoulder. "You know, I think Dad only came here because he had nowhere else to go before this new job started. I bet he's really lonely." I pull out the Polaroid of my dad that I took just a few hours ago. It's crazy how similar we look. "Do you think I'm like him?"

"No, Ruby. Your dad was afraid of a lot of things. But you're pretty fearless."

I don't feel fearless, or strong, or brave. I only feel tired. And a little sad. "I think I'm going to go to bed." I pack up Dad's box of stuff, and all my pictures from last night.

"Are you hungry? I could fix you something."

"Not really. But maybe we could have dinner tonight. Together."

Her face lights up. "I've just found a new recipe. It calls for okra. I don't even know what that is!"

I trudge upstairs and head into my bedroom. I strip off my Girl Scout costume and climb into the covers and close my eyes. And then open them.

I can't believe everything that's happened in the last few days. I'm not really sure what I'm supposed to do with all these memories, all these feelings I have. Before, I would have just pushed them out of my mind. But that doesn't feel right anymore. Sort of like the anti–Girl Scout badges I made, I want to wear what's happened on my sleeve. I don't want to forget any of it.

Even though I should go to sleep, I climb out of bed. I gather up all the pictures I've taken since my birthday. I collect Charlie's buttons. I rip off one of my Girl Scout badges. I take my dad's letter. I run upstairs to the attic and I get my old map. I hang it on the wall over my bed.

And then I attach everything to the map, covering over a quick sketch I make of a tree. My friends are the branches, even

Katherine. All the shots of my dad's blue truck I snapped in the parking lot become the leaves. I stick on Charlie's buttons like acorns. Everything gets put up like a collage. And right in the center of everything, I stick the picture Beth took of me on my birthday. It's covered in droplets of wax and melted ice cream, but you can still tell I'm smiling.

WOODLAND HIGH SCHOOL
800 N. MOSELEY DRIVE
STOCKBRIDGE, GA 30281
(770) 389-2784